Sharing

by

Richard J. Oddo

'A Spiritual Warrior'

First Edition ~ Jan. 1990

All essays, poems, parables and
stories are handwritten and edited
by the author

All artwork is hand drawn
by the author

Published by~ Richard J. Oddo
P. O. Box 7012
Halcyon, Ca. 93421

ISBN : 0-945637-02-0
Library of Congress Catalog Card # : 89-92801

Children of Eternity

Once one understands the meaning of their life, then what value does vocalizing the truth have? Once one lives in freedom, there is no necessity to expound the virtues of our cause. Once one is thoroughly convinced of their spiritual reality, then they can live no other priority.

To one who is living the truth, that one is my eternal companion, and even if our physical path never does cross, I still am one with that soul of freedom, and walk the very steps of their journey. We are the children of eternity, and commune within the same conscious light, sharing of the same heart as we sojourn within this miraculous realm together...

May I offer my humble gratitude to those who have shared love, and opened their heart to this wandering warrior, and bow in respect to their remembrance of divinity:

~Shree Maa ~ Swami Satya Nanda~
~Francesca ~ Nick ~ Swami E.C. ~
~Swami Shraddhananda ~
~Swami Bhaktimayananda ~
~Swami Ganeshananda ~ Steve ~
~Swami Atmarupananda ~ Kai King~

Dedication

Beyond name, beyond form, I
remember a truth – it is my
life, it is my breath; and
while I walk shadowed,
gazing in anticipation for the
light to flood me with love,
I nurture a communion
within my soul, and give it
as the flowering of my heart
to the essence of life eternal.
In humility I bow in reverence,
and with the greatest of love
and respect dedicate this
sharing of my heart to
'Mother', my life, my breath.

Table of Contents

About The Author ~
About The Artist ~
About The Caligrapher ~
About The Editor ~
About The Publisher ~

I was not born, I will not die.
I live everywhere; my education
is life. All my activities are
conscious explorations of freedom,
and I have nothing cute to say,
or profound dialogue to expound.
I walk with my eyes open and
my ears vigilant, for I am a
receiver of the gift of life. With
the greatest sincerity and
humility, I will respectfully
use this 'blessed gift, as a vehicle
to express physically the truth of
my spiritual nature, and thus
my life is a continuous prayer,
and my relationship to you is
a 'Sharing of The Heart'...

Message From My Heart

My book is not for the purpose of increasing knowledge and acquiring new concepts – it is just the opposite. It is my intention to lessen the complexity of thought, and provide inspiration for living the simplicity of freedom which is already in our possession. Man voluntarily gives his spiritual freedom away thru the acceptance of limiting dogma and stagnant conceptualization. I am one voice in thousands who shout the call of communion with our source – it is the freedom we are born with, and our heritage to claim. The responsibility to live the truth of our true spiritual nature lies with us, and no looking outward is possible. Look no further than yourself for your redemption, for salvation is your very heart, and love is the only forgiveness you need. Stand within the light of your source, and know that no other reality exists, for you are the light of God...

Granite or Crystal

The mind may be expansive, vibrant and unlimited, but words and books are not. There are a few hundred words that express the inner feelings of the heart, and every spiritual book contains these same words, mixed together in every conceivable order. There is only one truth, and each attempt to speak it or write it, is merely the re-ordering of the same overused, limited words. The same basic truth has been repeated thousands of times, by thousands of different souls, all thru the ages. In person they were able to convey a vibrant energy of life along with the words, but in a book this vital energy is missing, and must be supplied by the reader. Thus even if a book be full of truth, few will be able to understand it in its limited, dead form. So here I present another dead piece of literature, but within these pages I present my heart, with the hope that this dead book has energy vibration—for even though a rock be dead, it can still transfer energy if its form be of crystal. So within this dead treatise I have given my love and soul energy, in hope that my sincere, dedicated life of freedom as a spiritual warrior will be conveyed. May you find within these pages the love with which they were written, and a catalyst to spark your realization of the divinity that you are. And may this book not be as a dead piece of granite to you, but have the energy and vibrancy of a clear, pure crystal...

Love
123

Sharing of The Heart

These pages are not an impersonal letter cast to the wind, they are writings poured from my heart, lit in the spiritual communion of my soul, and offered as prayer to the beckoning of your heart. My eyes yearn for the vision & hold sacred in the treasuretrove of my longing — for & be a dreamer yearning for communion to blossom fragrant within this body of Man, much as his soul awakening beyond the shadows that blind his way in forgetfulness. How desperately & wish to see the concepts and judgement that holds us apart, melted asunder the overpowering light of love, and we joined into harmony to share of the truth that has birthed the soul of our divinity. It is inevitable that we will rise into higher light, so can & be faulted for giving all my love, energy and even my life to quickening this burgeoning seed of hope. Thus before you is not a book, but rather seeds of communion, and it be in your power to bring them to life with the tears of our love, and in compassion and strength nurture their growth within the fertile soil of your wisdom. This is the bonding & seek, and the reason & offer these pages to your heart, it is my soul crying forth thru all eternity, longing to share the truth, but forlorn in its attempt; yet hope springs eternal, and once again & bow in humility, and with respect and love offer these pages to you as a 'Sharing of The Heart'...

Art Plate 2-02 ~ Sharing of The Heart ~

11

Spiritual Equals

We are all equal spiritual beings of freedom, and there are no differences of color, sex or belief when it comes to our spiritual identity. The Absolute contains no aspects of conceptualization, no dualities, and no distinctions. We are spiritual essence within the Absolute, and even though in physical form of race and gender, the spirit within us all is the one, undiffering, pure Absolute. We are one family within the fabric of manifestation, and all humans are of the same brotherhood, no matter if they be man or woman. The biological differences are just for function, but the spirit which brings life to us all is beyond time, space, form, birth and death, and I see one and all as this divine aspect. But for convenience of writing, I will use the masculine gender in this book, but in all cases it is the intent of this author that both 'he' and 'she' be indicated. Both man and woman are exactly equal spiritual beings, and this simple realization is needed if harmony of human relations is ever to happen. There is no superiority of physical form, greatness comes thru living in spiritual realization, and both man and woman are exactly equal in opportunity to grasp the truth and live fully in its light. We each have within us the potential to rise to the highest light, it is our determination and sincerity which creates the possibilities, and the possibilities are limitless no matter who you are, for our reality be of God, and God be unbounded as the infinite dream of eternity.

A Spiritual Warrior

I call myself a spiritual warrior, yet I am dedicated to peace. My battle is personal, and at all times I am in a state of vigilance, as I fight the delusory ignorance of my worldly nature. We all abide within the world, but a spiritual warrior recognizes a higher nature within himself, and fights to maintain this realization moment by moment. My war is peaceful, and I am in no jeopardy of defeat, for my spiritual essence is the only reality; but the battle I wage is one of remembrance, so that I will not slip into delusion. I fight my own slothful ignorance within the battleground of manifested relativity, and the weapons I use are my sincerity and respect, and the war I wage is to realize my true self nature, and abide in the truth of its being. Gone are the days of weak acquiescence, an inner strength and courage are necessary to face a spiritual life. But just because I call myself a spiritual warrior, it doesn't mean I honor a spiritual concept you can relate to. My vision is inward, and my revelations unto myself, for I cannot be generalized or categorized – my individual expression is unique, and my relation to the world is in sharing this uniqueness. Thru deep reflection I have come to understand one fact – I am a spiritual being of freedom within the essence of the Absolute; and because I fight to maintain this realization, and live the simplicity of its truth, I humbly and respectfully call myself a spiritual warrior...

The Wilderness

Within these pages I often speak of the wilderness & explore, but since the majority of my readers are urban dwellers, perhaps a few words of explanation might help to preface my "Wanderings of The Heart."

I do not use the term 'wilderness' in a romantic sense, it is a term used to designate the lands that have been set aside by congress to remain in their virgin quality. Within most National Forests and other public lands there are vast areas of outstanding, rugged beauty that are protected from all intrusion – no roads, homes, buildings or industry; and man is only a visitor there, where foot or horseback is the only means of exploration. Though there are usually trails leading into its heart, most of the area remains untouched and rough in its pristine splendor.

These are the wilderness areas I refer to, and they vary incredibly in scope – from jagged mountain escarpents, to forested hills, to deep twisted canyons, to ocean bluffs, to giant redwood groves, to desert rock and rolling dunes. They are all so incredibly unique, and here is where I call home. I explore them all as the seasons permit, and because I am now well experienced, I spend most of my time off the trails walking across the terrain with no set course. My favorite pursuit is to climb rocky peaks that afford panoramic views of the surrounding area. I climb about 75 peaks a year, and walk about 2,000 miles in pure virgin territories, communing with the abundance of life, but more

14

importantly letting my true nature feel the pulse of pure experience.

Yes, there is danger in what I do. The mountains are always composed of loose rock and I do fall occasionally, and the winds rip me as I traverse the sheer mountain ridges, and I get hailed and rained on, making the rocks very slippery, and me shiver. Often I climb thru ice and snow to scale the peaks, and the lightening storms blast around me. And even though most people think bears, snakes and mountain lions are a big threat, actually the thorny bushes are my greatest adversaries, and the inconspicuous loose rock is what usually sends me catapulting (and I won't even mention about getting lost from time to time, or how occasionally I fall thigh deep in quicksand - ha, the list could go on and on into monotony).

Each terrain has its own type of difficulty, and now after eleven years of living amidst its beauty, I have found them to be more than just my home, but the actual breath of my soul, and the danger is just one facet of its varying personality, no different than the warmth of the sun, or the purity of its air and water. The incredible virgin beauty is one that has to be experienced to be understood - the explosion of Spring's flowers and fragrance, cascading waterfalls singing of love, crystalline lakes set in towering granite cirques, rock escarpments stretching thousands of feet straight into the sky, and the glorious view from atop the summit unfolding 100 miles of primordial beauty in every direction - the power and aliveness one feels embraced in Nature's arms is only possible to feel, and never explain in words.

Our nature is part of this primal orchestration, and only within its fold does one feel the very roots of what our true nature has embodied. This communion with raw life, as I walk amidst its dangerous and gently nature, is the very essence that brings life into perspective. Here there are no goals or paths to encumber the fleeting moment of eternity, no past or future to dictate one's actions, no desire or expectation to burden one's spirit, for here one's spirit can be pure in its freedom without a selfhood to bring separation. I don't go to the wilderness, I am the wilderness, and in walking its miraculous realm my spirit soars with the freedom of a spiritual warrior, for I am just one infinitesimal aspect of its virgin character, and part of the totality of its being — for here there are no desires of selfhood, and I can simply be what I am.

The author in his office, the wilderness — picture taken by Steve, a fellow warrior, at the 'Wonderland of Rocks' - March 88

Mother, God, The Absolute

There is an ultimate reality beyond manifest being – it is a pure, aware essence without name and form, and thus ungraspable and undefinable, & call this totality the 'Absolute'. It is the life factor within the cell of living structure, supporting all existence, yet has no structure of its own. It is pure awareness, as the original source beyond comprehension, and life is its dream.

The dream is bound within a relationship of relativity, manifested as the consciousness of self awareness. Thus name and form spring into being as life, in the recognition of itself. The dream is the totality of manifest expression, and thus it is the power of life expressed, so in my writings & will refer to this totality of living consciousness as God, for existence is our relationship of divinity where awareness has sprung as seed into life, and we as God, create thru consciousness the manifest expression, which provides a vehicle for us to experience the totality of our being – a dream unfolded that watches itself in the forgetfulness of its true nature of Godhood.

God is the relationship of relative being with that of pure awareness. We are not separate from God, for all of existence is the name and form of God, thus we are God, and so is everything. God is the very personality of our consciousness, thus we can establish a very personal relationship with God, and commune within this aware feeling.

It is our selfhood of God recognizing a truth beyond the limitation of manifest being, and immersing its God nature into its source. We are God, and can open our consciousness to the light that is the essence of our life. God is the totality of existence, and is the consciousness of communion in Self reflection of the Absolute, and we be the cells of this embodiment of life. But communion is the outpouring of love, thus no relationship is available with the ungraspable Absolute, but we can commune unto ourself thru the power of love in existence within the totality, and this oneness of life in communion is God.

Beyond name and form I know of my reality as existence Absolute; and within manifest expression I commune unto my Selfhood as God. And though my actuality as consciousness of God is the recognition that I am one with the divinity of the whole, there is a certain lack of personal feel in my heart in using the wording 'God.' So my heart demanded a more personal wording to convey my communion of love and the joy it expresses, so with the greatest of respect I call my union with life 'Mother'.

'Mother', 'God', 'Father' - it is all still a relationship within the totality of our Self, communing unto our divinity as the sacred thread that binds us to existence Absolute. But is this not the most personal experience possible, the actual recognition of being life in the miracle of existence? thus 'Mother' is reflective of this power and tenderness of life, blossoming into the void, eternal and infinite, reaching beyond, and cloaked in mystery.

Mother is the living truth manifested into consciousness, and holds embodied within Her totality all essence of life issued as awareness from the Absolute. To me, Mother is not a personality, diety or concept, and is beyond the terms commonly used as 'Mother Nature', or the many Goddesses termed as 'holy Mother', or 'The Mother'. 'Mother' is the encompassing God, and no gender or form is suggested – Mother is God in existence as the living expression of the Absolute, and everything is embraced within the purity of Mother's awareness; thus our consciousness can establish a very personal relationship with its true Self, and live in the remembrance of our unity as Mother.

So in truth I have established a pilgrim's path of devotion with my Godhood, and term this a prayer to Mother. I live the remembrance of my divinity, and have the blissful joy of communing in relationship with my Godhood – it is all the wondrous play of Mother, and the miracle of the Absolute. And I? well I am just a dream character of self consciousness, dancing in the pure awareness of a dream called Mother, and within the living tissue is the Dreamer, the undifferentiated, undefinable, ungraspable Absolute.

Art Plate 2-03 ~ Embrace of Love ~

Ever so softly my spirit embraces me,
my anxious fears melted by love.
Oh so tender I hear the voice of my Self,
and know I am life eternal.
Throughout eternity
I have wandered from home,
separated by my forgetfulness.
But I cannot stray
from my reality of divinity,
and the echo of God
is my very breath.
So I will dance
in the curiosity of my ignorance,
and think I have traveled so far,
but Mother/Father holds me close,
and the gentle whisper
is my very soul...

There is a fearful selfhood, anxious and
suspicious of the concepts it creates. Fear
surrounds the ignorance of its forgetfulness,
for it has journeyed far from home, and now
must defend an ego it created, and oh how
vulnerable is this infant of curiosity and
desire. Ever clutching at attainment, and so
fearful of life, for its vision cannot reach
past the inevitability of death. But in truth
we are not this child, our reality is a spiritual
nature that stretches to the infinity of existence
absolute. Our true self is that Father/Mother
principle of eternal life, and is manifest of
our true nature of absolute being. With
wisdom and compassion we sooth the child
of manifest, ever guiding a truer way, and
always present within the spiritual heart.
For we are life eternal, and all expression
is but our children of curiosity.

20

Art Plate 2-04 ~ Child of Mother ~

Forged in the fire of deep conviction,
the long years of dedication
built strength of integrity enduring,
opening my heart
into communion of its source.
It is love in remembrance of love,
and as child I am accepting,
recognizing a truth
ever present in my heart.
Exuberant is my joy,
respect blossoming into life
blessed eternal by Mother.
Yet this pilgrim wanders deeper,
down a corridor fragrant
with the blooming of humility,
for love shows oneness
set delicately in balance,
nurtured by a loving hand.
Yet deeper the heart ever yearns,
a pilgrim's blessed boon,
opening wider to infinite grace,
committed in personal truth
to ideals held sacred,
sincerity the prayer
as living breath of life eternal.
Though the way be strewn
with rocks of useless attachment,
sincerity always finds a course
like water pouring forth,
cascading into the purity of oneness.
Life be miracle, a bond sacred,
and to be Mother's living light,
aware of truth held live, enfolding death,
bestows communion immersed in our source;
this be the prayer of freedom,
and the living love and breath of life,
for now we be the child
held in Mother's eternal embrace...

Art Plate 2-05 ~ Truth's Embrace ~

We are embraced by a compassionate strength which whispers the truth of life's miracle. In acceptance we allow ourself to remember our heart, and follow its words of silence. We are the eyes and ears of our spiritual reality, and firmly are we held in the arms of life eternal. The manifest form is an expression of the true nature of our being, and how wondrous it is to behold the grace of life, and be its living breath of freedom. To walk this realm of mystery and wonder is the dream of our spirit, and perpetual remembrance must always be focused on the reality of our essence, which holds a form dear till it draws the consciousness of separation back into its oneness again. We are the conscious awareness of God, as God actualized into living expression, and though we embrace but a shadow of the true reality, we still are essence of one totality, and in this oneness none be separated from eternal truth.

Wanderings of The Heart

Weminuche Wilderness ~ July 1986 ~

Though craggy rock escarpments demand my heart, and the wondrous flower displays and whispering aspen groves speak so clear of love, within colorado's shinning light it is the incredible abundance of wildlife that brings my avenue of greatest communion. All of Earth is my home of communion, but I can recognize a quickening of heart when my path leads where I may chance upon other lives of dynamic movement. Every crevice, every cave, behind each stone and hidden in the trees lie the animals of the wilderness, and there still exists those virgin spots that are strongholds for these dearest of lives; and there I travel in their land, a land much like a canvas and they the living paint, and I walk as viewer of this artistry, yet also the creator of its bend and flow.

Upon a dirt road, 8,000 feet up into the forested hills, I parked boardering the Weminuche Wilderness, and here I started my ascent up a creek that flowed thru a field of fragrance, for glorious the flowers profusely bloom in the high country of colorado. The sun bathed me in warmth as I ascended the lower slopes on route to the rocky main ridge 3,000 feet above.

My course brought me up a steep grassy incline that stretched into a broad, open field dotted with pines and firs. The lush plateau was blazing with wildflowers, but what got my immediate attention was the presence of well over 100 elk contentedly grazing on the bountiful dew drenched grass. It seemed that none had noticed how I suddenly popped up from the steep slope onto the meadow, for none even looked my way. Closest to me was a gathering of mothers surrounding their spotted calves, with the nearest being about 25 feet away; and scattered throughout the trees and along the hillside were stately bull elk adorned with a magnificent armoring of antlers. Oh so many herds of elk I have been graced to see, but to stand in their midst as they serenly browsed was a true blessing indeed. Eventually the herd moseyed into the densely forested mountainside, and I sent my gratitude and love with them, and happily unfroze from my statue like posture and continued up the ridge.

My destination at last reached, I found a flat rock to serve as throne for my grand view of the vast expanse of valleys that lay 5,000 feet below, but mainly the view I sought was of the awesome peaks of 'The Needles', rising in defiance north of my ridge. The Needles are a grouping of 14,000 foot peaks which rise to pin point jagged summits, and their foreboding chacacter inspires visions of rugged adventure in areas far remote to man's intrusion. What joy to see this virgin beauty stretching unimpeded to the horizon and beyond. And up there the heralder of the sky, as I looked above to watch a solitary hawk carve circles in his domain of beauty. How serene and powerful is his flight of freedom, and his presence drew me higher into that consciousness.

Always with reluctance I leave the high country of expanded view, for it broadens my perception of this vast realm, and my awareness of perspective within it. But I am a creature with itchy feet, so down the ridge I descended crossing one field after another blanketed with purple flower stocks from wild onions, intermingled with red indian paintbrush and florescent yellow daisys. Suddenly a coyote leaped from the tall grass, and bounded off in large arching leaps across the meadow. I figured she probably ran from her den, so I purposely changed my course so as not to get to close to her cubs.

The change of direction proved to be an incredible blessing, for I had only gone a ¼ mile when out of the tall grass in front of me a spotted fawn jumped up and ran about 12 feet, and then stopped to see what had caused the noise that alerted it. But I had already froze in my position, assuming the stoic posture of an old, dead tree stump. The fawn listened intently for 5 minutes, but since it detected no movement it began to relax and walk around nibbling grass. Even though I was but 15 feet away, it is movement and noise that alert deer, so there I stood as frozen statuary while this beautiful little Bambi nibbled around me.

After a while it went back to where it had been lying, and bent its head down and started nozzling and licking something in the tall grass about 10 feet away. Suddenly another fawn stood up, and cute as could be these two little deer rubbed faces, and then both started

28

nibbling grass and walking around me. I
sent such love out to them, and the wonder
of this splendid opportunity to commune
in this vibrantly alive realm. But my
attention was drawn away from my
reverie back to the nesting spot where
the two fawns had lain.

I thought I detected some movement, and
sure enough to my utter amazement, I saw
some ears twitching, and then a very tiny,
new born fawn stood up. Oh how precious
this little one was, as it stretched and
yawned, and then began to wobbly
walk around. It was too small to be
born when the others were, so it must
have been that two does left their
fawns together while they foraged. I would
have loved to hold and caress them, but
I held as still as a rock, uncomfortably
balanced on one foot. With three of them
walking circles all around me, I had
no chance to be unobserved for a second
to assume a more comfortable position;
but this occasion was so rare that I
didn't care, and all I could do was
melt into the exuberant joy I felt for
the miracle enfolding me.

For over an hour I communed with
this incredible event, as the three Bambis'
browse all around me not paying the
slightest attention to my presence, but
the dying sun told me it was time to
continue down the mountain. I was
reluctant to move for fear of scaring
the fawns, so I moved ever so slowly,
but realized that this process would
take hours to be out of their sight, so
I finally decided to take a few normal
steps and hope for the best. As I took
my first few steps I observed them

29

closely, and to my surprise they showed no alarm at all, only curiosity and surprise — it was as if they were puzzled why this firmly planted tree now decided to uproot itself and walk away. Finally I was 100 feet away, and they still were just standing there staring at me, so in gratitude I sent my love and gave thanks to our spirit of oneness, and continued on home in a reverie of approaching twilight.

My van was parked with a clear view to the west, so as I gratefully partook of a delicious salad, I was able to watch the sun put on a spectacular show of blending and melting colors. How wondrous is the sky, it is the canvas supreme, and each evening the sun paints a glorious array of dancing patterns, and lets our imagination intertwine into its realm of dying embers, just to have the stars peek back at us like all the countless eyes that compose the life of our soul, and speak to us of the immensity unfolded that is this realm we so blessedly create. For hours I could do no more than watch as one vision faded into another form, and each one so entirely captivating, yet only shadows of the reality of our nature. So I watched in fascination at the miracle of our existence and allowed it to weave its tapistry of form, which so mysteriously echos and traps our consciousness.

Later that night I lay in bed gazing at the stars thru my skylights, giving thanks in meditative joy, when I began to hear a noise outside my van. I wanted to dismiss this intrusion upon my reverie of reflection and stay in my contemplative communion of joy, but the noise made its presence known, so now it was time to focus on a new experience. So I grabbed my flashlight and went outside to investigate the strange chewing like noise. I looked around my van, but the noise now appeared to be coming from the area of an old closed road. At the entrance of the road was a gate, and I flashed my light at its base, but the noise was higher, so I raised my light up, and perched on top of the 4 foot gate was a large, plump porcupine chewing a hole in the 'road closed' sign. I had to laugh heartily as the porcupine stood there, surprised I'm sure, blinking its big, gentle eyes at me; and then it woddled across the top of the gate and with difficulty slowly climbed down, and shuffled its quills as it disappeared into the bushes. It had chewed quite a large hole in the road sign, and as my other encounters with porcupines attest, they are always chewing on the strangest things.

I once again settled into bed, and gazed upon the stars of my consciousness. How incredible the astounding variety of life, and each captured within its own relative world, and yet we as the joint creation of consciousness are living a relationship within one totality. Our values, hopes, goals and desires differ so completely in this realm; and here our paths intermingle, and yet our perceivable world is of a different relationship for each arena of consciousness, that varies with its predestined form of perspective. As much as I wished to commune with all the variety of life I witnessed that day,

I was still only an intruder venturing within the limits of my mind. But my heart was open and pure, so there was a bond of relationship, even though the aspirations of the individual forms may have differed. As my heartfelt predilection, I can only recognize our unity and joyously abide in the reality that brings oneness to all the astonishing expressions of life I behold, and know that my love will find its communion beyond the limitations imposed by my understanding, for all of life is but one reality, and communion be its very breath, and love its undying soul.

Art Plate 2-06 ~ Gentle Whisper ~

Parable - Moon in the Pool

Two Vedic priests were sitting by a lovely lotus pond one evening. The moon was full and filling the night with a silvery luminescence, and the pond itself reflected the bright form of the radiant moon. One priest wistfully commented, "the reflection is just like our true nature, shining brightly beyond touch, yet still there." Suddenly a splash rent ripples thru the pond as the reflected image of the moon was shattered into isolated spots of wavy light. "It is not as our true nature," the other priest replied, "so easily & disrupt its form, while the moon remains. Just like the moon's reflection, your form is but illusion, and everything outside of us is but delusion of the mind. Your true nature is not in the mind, but is in fact the essence which gives the mind awareness. You are one with Reality, and your true Self is the essence of its manifest form. If you feel you can look outward and abide in that form, then you will be looking for a silvery moon captured inside a pond, and thus every ripple of delusion will shake your conceptual idea of what your true nature really is. Do not look to reflections, you are the very fact itself."

Art Plate 2-07 ~ Sharing Eternity ~

How precious is life, and the desire
to accept it. We are not here to
achieve, but rather to accept the
mystery and blessing of life's
unfoldment, and share this gift of
miracle in a relationship of spiritual
priority; and be not deceived by the
tumultuous activity surrounding you,
for there is no other priority in life
obligating you. You are free and must
allow yourself to accept this freedom,
and extend it to all those around you;
thus we can share our love
unconditionally and stop limiting
ourself to a physical expression of fear
and doubt. We are a spiritual being of
miracle and wonder, and life is our
vehicle to express divinity in this
moment of infinite awareness; and in
this higher light of consciousness we
can bestow upon the blooming youth
a heritage of wisdom, for spiritual
remembrance is the only testimony to
a life marked by eternity. All else
falls to dust, but communion with
your source is an epitaph written by
the eternal hand, and carries the
fragrance of life beyond life.

Art Plate 2-08 ~ Sharing Divinity ~

Sharing light, sharing love, it is a gift, and even more so a blessing that brings our heart into remembrance, and thus communion is divinely embraced. Sharing brings a higher awareness where one purposely subjugates their individual selfhood, and merges into their true self, by realizing their oneness with the one being served. It is love in harmony, where both are immersed in divine unity; a marriage equal in gift, for the bond be a joining within the heart, reaching far beyond physical expression, to the very soul of our purpose. The mind cannot guide in service, it is the heart that leads this path of love, for only thru the inspiration of the heart can service be shared with enthusiasm, yet wisdom need always be present to direct the heart from wasting precious energy, and setting a course that insures value. Sharing is an art for both giver and received, for subtle is the balance when communion be the goal. But love cannot stray far when sharing fosters spiritual growth, for the light of realization shines equal when unity is achieved in the bonds of a communion divine. Give of your heart, and find that you are the one blessed by your love, for it is spiritual law that the giver receives, and so does all the universe.

Wanderings of The Heart

Mt. Saint Helens ~ After the Eruption ~

Mt. St. Helens had just blasted its top off in one of the most awesome displays of destruction modern man has ever seen. So while the ground was still sizzling hot and violently scarred I journeyed into its back country to see the incredible power the Earth just unleashed. The destruction was amazing, but sadly all life had been destroyed over the entire mountain, and the trees were laid flat in orderly patterns for a vast surrounding area, blown down by the force of the tremendous blast. Here was the rare opportunity to walk the earth primordial, for it was forming itself anew, remembering its dream of virgin, lush beauty. The bleakest desert is a paradise in comparison to the total depravation of life after the devastation, and it emanates a feeling like walking upon the moon where life is foreign to its nature.

But the eruption was but a passing moment of eternity, and with each passing instant life once again reclaims the devastated ground as its nurturing home. And as the Earth revolves, eons will pass and once again the mountain valley that surrounds the bleak escarpment of Mt. St. Helens will be teeming in life abundantly displaying a rich beauty man can relate to.

But for now I had the rare opportunity to walk its primal land of destruction. The vision it brought forth was from a book by Tolkien ~ for I could envision this vast bleakness as the destruction of the fire breathing dragon from the Hobbit, and it brought Middle Earth into a vision I could now relate to.

I set out hiking thru some of its former valleys and lakes, but because of the enormous mud flows that were unleashed when the tremendous heat melted the snow on its crest, I found no lakes but only mud ponds, and it was impossible to discover where the valleys had been. The flowing mud, which was now drying, had carved deep ravines and ridges everywhere, totally changing the original way water had flowed. I was always walking hundreds of feet above or below where the original surface of the earth had been, with no vegetation to be found.

My walk was fascinating, but it was also very depressing to see all the vibrant life destroyed, so I set a course toward June Lake where I felt its distance might have saved it. June lake was still mostly intact, with trees and bushes still standing and the surrounding cliffs unblemished, but the mud flow had crossed very close to it and had filled in the lake completely. But Mother Earth was now rebuilding, and the three large waterfalls that flowed into the lake basin had created a shallow pond. The water was only a foot deep, but it covered the entire surface of the basin, giving it a beautiful, shimmery effect. If I didn't turn in the direction of St. Helens, than the view of the lake and cliffs was a very lovely sight. Three gorgeous waterfalls fell into the lake from the surrounding cliffs, which reached upward 600 feet.

My time at the lake was peaceful and the air serenely still, but my curiousity was constantly aroused by one strange phenomenon. Two of the waterfalls came from cliff areas that had obvious valleys initiating the source of the flowing water, but the third waterfall was an enigma, for it seemed to come out of a vast cliff that stretched up 500 feet, and I was continually puzzled how the water could suddenly cascade into the lake without a canyon feeding the flow. I had trees blocking most of my view of the cliff, so I never could get a real good look, and kept telling myself there must be some hidden channel I couldn't see. But my curiousity finally won and I walked to the top of a ridge on the far side of the lake, and sure enough the cliff had no upper valley or gully, but instead I could clearly see a cave that the water came rushing out of.

The cave was only 75 feet above the level of the lake, but below the cave was a very dense growth of thickly thorned bushes, and the angle of the cliff was quite steep. But regardless, I just had to investigate, for it is a rare sight indeed to see a stream gush forth from a cave. But first I had to cross the lake, and even though it was shallow, the mud was uncomfortably deep. So I floated my way across on half submerged logs that were in the lake, and hopped from one to another, almost falling in continuously~ I looked like a man dancing on fire instead of water. But I finally reached the other side about 100 feet to the right of the cascading creek and 75 feet below the cave. But getting to it was not going to be easy, as a matter of fact it was going to be down right suicidal, for the slope was so steep I couldn't climb it, and the bushes were so thickly covered with large, long thorns that they would impale me if I fell into them, and the loose ground covering the slope was wet and muddy. It had all the conditions to create a nightmere for climbing, but I was determined to go and sat back figuring a way.

I got back from the slope aways and figured the best possible course, and then I looked for a strong stick about 5 feet long and 3 inches thick. My plan was simple, so I set out to tempt my fate. I would take the staff and with both hands drive it into the muddy slope 18 inches above me, then I'd put one foot at a time above the base of the stick— sort of forming my own stairs. Then I'd wiggle my feet till I felt fairly well grounded, and then pull the staff out and jam it into the slope above me, and once again lift one foot at a time to the staff's base, and try desperately to balance myself while I attempted to pull the stick out of the mud, so I could repeat the process. It was a very tedious effort, and after I reached 40 feet up the danger became very obvious. Falling down the slope was not a life and death matter, for I would have slid on the wet, loose soil, but that is not all that lay below me; I had a beautiful, lush bed of 2 inch thorns to land in that would definitely use me as a pin cushion. The ground was so damp that many times as I tried to raise my feet up to the level of the staff, the stick would break loose and my shoulders would smack up against the slope. My feet only broke loose one time, and I would have fallen 50 feet into the waiting arms of my thorny brothers, but for once the stick held firm and I managed to pull myself up. As a matter of fact, the staff held so firm that when I got above it I could barely pull it out of the slope, and almost lost my balance in trying. But the tedious process continued on, foot by foot, working my way diagonally toward my destination.

It was incredible, I finally reached the cave and it was indeed an amazing sight. The cave was only 4 feet high and 2 feet wide, but out of its gaping mouth issued a flow of crystal clear water that plummeted to the lake below. I was able to stand on a rock outcropping at the mouth of the cave surrounded by a lush growth of flowers and ferns. I had never seen anything of this nature, and just stood there in awe at the beauty of this magnificient sight. I placed my hands into the cave and let the water run over them, grasping handfuls of crystaline life and splashing it on my face and neck. How invigorating it felt to taste the reward that I had risked my life for.

How reflective are our endeavors, for in that moment of pure innocents my life was no more than the flow of that crystal stream, issuing forth from unseen sources and cascading down the rocky course of consciousness, just to join within the tranquility of

the still water of my true essense
which is one with all existence. I
laughed and sang of life's simplicity,
and once again was given a lesson of
the ways of a spiritual warrior. Life
itself is the challenge, and its very
essense is what we drink of, thus
purpose is provided by the experience of
this unfolding moment. We need not
seek our Self, for we are simply that
which is.

Art Plate 2-09 ~ Harmony ~

I sit in peace,
and the grass grows by no effort of mine.
Life is a miraculous explosion,
and it needs not my hand
to set its course.
I sit here in peace,
yet all is being done.
The water serenely flows,
the breeze gently flutters my clothes.
The ground I sit upon is firm,
for truth is the strength of my foundation,
and life expressed is self evident,
needing no discovery or explanation.
My eyes are closed
to search of myself,
for in communion
my true nature is the Reality,
and it needs no ignorant selfhood
to look for its light.
I sit in peace
in the truth of my God nature,
and let the grass grow
in its God nature.
Reality provides a stage of consciousness
where all is in harmony,
and I need but walk in serenity
and allow nature to be itself,
with no attempt of mine
to alter or control it.
At peace I sit
and watch the grass grow,
and the birds fill
this realm of miracle with song;
and ever so soon
I join the oneness of Mother's love,
but for this brief moment of eternity,
I sit in peace
and watch the grass grow.

45

Art Plate 2-11 ~ Life's Balance ~

Tenderly imbue the fragrance of the flower, and now the essence is part of your being, it is absorbed into your fiber and becomes your very strength. It is the fragrance of love bestowed, and so graciously your heart receives its gift and respectfully makes this sharing of life its own. It is the same with all of creation — it is the balance of gift and received, the sharing of soul within physical expression. Closely observe the harmony, it is the miracle beyond mind. Within your very life is the breath of all creation, for all existence is one reality. Your actions are not separate unto themselves, all life is inter-related into one whole — the light of the sun is your energy, and each flowing stream is your living essence. We are sharing one awareness in infinite forms and degrees of expression, and to abide in communion with this oneness of life brings the love and joy of spiritual realization. Mystery lies hidden as the miracle unfolds, so accept the fragrance of this blossoming of life, and this acceptance of blessings is the very life of that which has so graciously given of itself — thus the life of creation is in bestowing life, for in sharing it is the giver that receives the love expressed, and both giver and received are necessary for communion. This is the cycle of life's wondrous miracle — the giver receives life, and in this remembrance we find communion within truth, and understand our nature of God as one Reality, and we be the expression of love realizing our self.

47

Art Plate 2-12 ~ Respect ~

Does respect only come with age, as one approaches the gate of death? Of course not, respect is a communion with life, not a fear of death. Age is no factor to determine sincerity, but experience can build a foundation for wisdom to be nurtured. But it is not necessary to understand life to have respect and love for its miracle of expression, it can only add to the depth, but anyone can feel the power of life and commune into the heart of its consciousness. It takes but the stilling of one's thoughts, for when concepts are dropped the world is self evident as the same essence as your own. Realization is remembrance of our oneness, and in this understanding of the equal nature of life in expression, respect is but communion within ourself, as divine consciousness in recognition of its Godhood. Just to witness the grandeur of life in the full awareness of what we truly are, as God-Absolute in miraculous expression, must bring a humbling respect for our relationship within this vast totality of God's manifest consciousness. How joyous it is to be a child of remembrance, awed by the miracle, humbled by our opportunity, and ever so deeply respectful of walking this sacred ground of our heart.

49

Parable ~ If The Shoe Fits

There was a minister who journeyed to a remote area of Africa to help bring spiritual understanding to the natives. The native people there were very small in stature, but were very understanding of simple truth.

The minister brought only the barest of necessities, for he didn't want to stand out, or appear to be materialistic. So he wore only shorts, and lived in a simple hut and ate the natives food. He would help in all their activities, and try to show by his example that he was devoted to his ideal of God, and had brotherly love for all the people.

One day a European passed by the village, and was greeted warmly and given food. As a gesture of gratitude he left a pair of fine leather boots. The chief called everyone together to decide who should have the boots, but since the boots were far to large to fit the small statured village people, the chief decided that the minister should have the boots. The minister immediately refused, saying, " I cannot accept these fancy boots. None of you have shoes, so you will think I'm prideful to have such fine possessions - I want to be just like everyone else." The chief smiled at the minister and explained, " if the boots fit then wear them. Do you think we judge your heart by what you wear? To wear boots or not wear boots will not bring us to respect you. anyone here would wear these boots if they fit, for the boots are only an object, and it does not make someone better to have an object. If a person has pride to have objects, than that person is worse off, and he loses respect, not gains it. But we make no virtue out of poverty, or a sin out of wealth – it is the heart that we look at, not the objects. Each of us has objects that we use, this is OK, but if we try to get more than we can use and think this will bring us respect, then we are a fool and only bring dishonor to ourself, and those around us feel shame in our presence. You are a fine man with a good heart, and this is why we respect you. Do not fear to have the things you need, for humility is not is doing without, humility is in sharing your love."

~ Meditate on This ~

The greatest king has no throne, for freedom is the measurer of true wealth...

~   ~   ~

Let your respect be demonstrated, like being a guest in your own home...

~   ~   ~

Life is too precious to analyze – if you must have answers, then listen in silence...

Wanderings of The Heart

Hoover Wilderness ~ Oct. 1985 ~

A great deal of the motivation for traversing the rugged wilderness is not only the astounding beauty, and experiencing the pristine virgin quality of our once primal land, but also to drink of the solitude it offers. My exploration is partly for physical isolation from the interference of distracting influences, so I can commune with my true nature and feel the pulse of the vibrant earth that nurtures me, and the wilderness brings renewal of purpose by the desolate nature of its raw inspiration.

The Hoover wilderness provides extraordinary beauty in the form of lush aspen laden valleys that stretch up into the pines, where waterfalls cascade from the magnificient glacier covered peaks. My hike that day had no special destination but to reach up into those lofty summits, and sit amongst the solitude of their powerful presence. The valley floor rose at a steady incline, with luminescent groves of aspen, bright with falls changing colors, separated by azure blue lakes and thick, lush emerald meadows, dripping with mornings crystal dew. From the ridges on either side cascaded huge ribbons of water from the extensive snow masses, and straight ahead lay the valley cirque where the granite rose abruptly to the high pass above, which was surrounded by the enormous peaks of the Sierras, heavily ladened with fresh snow from its last violent confrontation with wet air masses.

    I was fortunate to have a good trail to ascend the cirque to the pass above, but as I looked far up the trail, about 1000 feet above me I saw a huge group of people plodding up the steep passage way. Well I happen to have a preference not to follow herds of cattle, sheep, pigs, goats or humans, so I picked up my pace and within a half hour managed to pass up this slow moving herd of humanity. It is strange (and rare) to see such large groups in the wilderness terrain, but this day was destined to teach me a lesson about such onslaughts.

    I reached the pass above, which still had large snow areas glistening in the bright sun, and there were several pretty, little lakes off a ways at the base of a large peak. So I hiked to their rock encrusted shore, and found a large slab of granite to lay on and bask in the sun. But all of a sudden I heard the march of humanity intruding into my sanctum of pristine beauty. It seemed my spot of communion was to be the destination of this horde of lowlanders who had ascended these mountain reaches. So I looked around and thought, 'where is the one place these disciples of racketous chattering won't go.' Well stretching to the limits of the sky above me was Excelsior Peak (12,446 feet), with a magnificent crag of rocks adorning its lofty summit. I had no intention of being in sight or ear shot of my noisy group of mountain truggers, so straight up the side of Excelsior's rocky flank I went.

I kept up a hard clip, and within an hour I reached its inspiring crest — the view was simply spectacular, and stretched unimpeded for over 50 miles in every direction. The awesome 14,000 foot peaks of the Sierras stretched to the south with Yosemite to the west, and the sublime vision of Mono lake lay 6,000 feet below to the east; everywhere my eyes beheld the beauty of granite captured lakes, cascading rivers, hanging glaciers, and colorful patches of aspens. What a glorious spot on my beloved Earth, and I found a flat piece of its peak to nest upon and serenely bask in the beauty of its grace, and soak in the grandeur of its panoramic vision as I communed in silence.

An hour of this blissful serenity drifted by, when suddenly I heard the huffing and puffing of exhausted homo sapians. I opened my eyes and to my amazement, rising over a lower crest was the human mass I had left far below. As snails on sticky cement they inched their way up to my tranquil spot of spiritual exuberation. Soon I was as an unseen rock being trampled upon by the parade of gasping enthusiasts. Click, click, click went off a dozen cameras recording proof of their daring, and out came a peak register from a pile of rocks that I had given no notice. Names and addresses were quickly filed in systematic order, congradulations were issued by the hearty survivors, and off went the hoary hoard down the peak without so much as anyone sitting silent to soak in the rapture of the rarified air, and

bask in the beauty of this awesome
expanse of pristine wilderness. One
man did look down at his feet, where
I was shaded by the density of the
dizzy group, and said 'sorry for the
intrusion' — ah, a spark of awareness.
And I did catch that this was a
mountaineering club, and that these
outtings are part of their regular affair.

I think it is marvelous that city
dwellers ban together to inspire each
other to venture out into wilderness
areas, but how much more benefit
they would derive if someone was in
their group who has a communion with
this virgin soil, and who could humbly
show them the respect this miraculous
realm deserves. Only thru a deeper
communion would they receive the gift
of serenity of soul, as well as a
purified physical body. But each of us
must procede at our own pace, and
even though I tried to avoid being caught
in their trample, I was glad that they
were living higher ideals suited to
their nature, and were earnestly
making an attempt.

The moral of my episode is that
one cannot avoid the world. That by
my very attempt to run away I drew
the world with me. One must be
secure in their realization wherever
they are blessed to be, and let the
world march on past as they serenely
watch in wonder. Avoidance is like a
magnet, and will draw the very thing
one is trying to obscure. Run to the
furthest cave in search of solitude,
and there you will find archeologists
investigating its walls and spelunkers

55

exploring its depths.

Thru various incidences I have been taught this repeatedly, and how fortunate that the lessons were usually humorous. I can recall one high adventure in the Pecos Wilderness of New Mexico (Aug 86). I was parked on the Pecos river and had climbed most of the peaks in the area, but the toughest one still lay virgin to my feet. It was straight up from where I surveyed its lofty summit, a full 4,800 feet towering above me, with snow and cliffs surrounding its jagged peak. But here was an opportunity to grasp a daring adventure, and find a virgin peak of utter solitude, so off I set thru the forest that blanketed the base of Santa Fe Baldy (12,636 feet), crossing numerous streams and isolated snow patches. The areas of snow gathered strength as I climbed each thousand feet, till finally after ascending 4,000 feet I was walking on top of six or more feet of snow, and falling in occasionally to add to the sport. But much tougher was what lay ahead, for in front of me now stood a 300 foot vertical wall of rock and ice, with a gorgeous frozen lake at its base. Slowly I proceeded, using all the rock climbing skills I had, and sadly they were insufficient for this difficult assult of its rock face, for the ice proved to be very treacherous. Several times I looked down and wondered why I picked such a crazy way to attempt this peak, but on I climbed till I finally reached an ice wall just 20 feet below the summit. I couldn't stop now, so hanging over the cliff & carved my way up the ice to the top in a sheer lunatic fashion.

But & made it, the peak was mine. Quiet, pristine and beautiful, and ah what solitude & should enjoy atop this formidable foe. But what's that & hear?, could it be the sound of running feet. My view had been of the cliff area and its ice lakes, but now & turned to the opposite side where & had no idea of its terrain, and before me lay a thinly forested gentle slope. Sure enough & saw two attractive, young ladies clad in teeshirt and shorts jogging up a trail that led right to where & stood. & watched with my mouth hanging open, flabbergasted at the sight. Within a minute they reached me and stood there beaming with pride, congradulating each other over their victory. & stumbled a few words out like, "what the heck are you two doing up here?" "Oh we're put of a running team that has competitive runs up the peak," they answered, "you'll be seeing lots of people real soon." Sure enough within 15 minutes & was surrounded by 35 people huffing and puffing, all wearing shorts while & had on snow gear and a pack. "But & climbed up a 4,800 foot cliff area", & ventured out, and which brought tremendous laughter. "There is a paved road on the other side", they announced, "just 2000 feet down, with a good trail to the top, and Santa Fe Baldy is the most widely climbed peak around." In shatters & slowly descended the ice and rock as laughter paved my way. But that

57

laughter has become a vehicle of joy that I now ride, and I cease to be amazed by the incredible play perpetrated upon my poor, beleaguered physical body.

Or perhaps the time I was exploring the Russian Peak Wilderness (July 85) will show how bizarre the world can become, when chasing pilgrims who are running for sanctuary. I purposely picked a very isolated wilderness area, and to make absolutely sure I would see no intruding humans I hiked off its trail system to a remote area of rugged character. Upon its bony crest I found a peak of outstanding viewing. Dropping on either side of this backbone ridge were cascading canyons that fell abruptly 5,000 feet to the lush plains below. Ah what peace, quiet and serenity I had enfolding me in this cocoon of tranquil communion, and there I stood mesmerized by the panorama, drinking in rapture, of its glorious vision.

But what is that dot I see way down in the valley — a building?, a field? — no, I think it's growing in size — a duststorm? But it keeps growing, and yes I can now make out an outline. Well I'll be darn, if it's not an airplane coming straight up the canyon at enormous speed — it's a fighter jet, and boy is he moving. The canyon rose very quickly to the ridge, and the jet was coming upward at a very sharp angle. Well I'm not unhospitable to a passing stranger, so I began to wave my arms frantically so he could see me. I was standing at the very top of the crest, and the side he approached on was a rugged slope, but the other side had a sheer 500 foot verticle cliff, and I stood just a foot or two from its edge. The jets course was right over my head by 50 feet, and I could see the pilot's face as he looked down at me while I waved in friendship. So as he zoomed on by he tilted his wings back and forth, and then did a complete roll as he disappeared into the sky. What a spectacular show, and I stood at the edge of the cliff waving goodbye. But it never dawned on me that jet planes usually travel in pairs, and as I stood totally focused looking in the direction the jet had gone, a second jet went blasting right over my head at enormous speed, throwing such a wave of power and surprise at me that I was pushed toward the 500 foot cliff. Desperately I tried to gain my balance as I pivoted on one foot, with the rest of my body leaning frantically over the edge of the abyss, with my arms flailing trying to grasp the invisible hand of Mother. I'm sure the second pilot had seen the first pilots actions and was just joking around, but my life hung on a fragile thread there, and once again the futility of running from humanities lacking consciousness showed itself in life scraping humor.

And perhaps one last illustration as the ultimate audacity to a poor pilgrims search for blessed solitude. The Granite Chief Wilderness is so unknown that even the rangers could not tell me of its location, but I found a trail covered in snow that

indeed led into its wilderness terrain
(Sept 85). My intent was to scale the
formidable Granite Chief peak, but after
eight miles of deep snow and ice covered
creeks, I came upon a towering edifice
of sheer rock and ice that stood
unconquerable on this frozen day.

Oh well, I guess I could find something
else less suicidal. Looking around I saw
to the east a massive giant of snow,
and what really intrigued me was there
appeared to be a little wood cabin at the
top. Being a romantic, my mind was
immediately filled with visions of a
wise old hermit who would share the
secrets of the universe, so off I galloped.

The incline was steady and sharp, as
I trudged thru deep snow straight up
the mountains flank. But now the
little cabin really appeared to be much
larger, like a fire lookout tower; well
that's OK, I'll meet a nice ranger out
here in the middle of nowhere who can
point out the names of all these
desolate peaks. So on I climbed thru
ever deepening snow, but a challenge
was started and my integrity was at
stake. The mountain steepened and I
had to use a staff up its icy slope,
but oddly the structure above didn't
appear to be a fire tower afterall, but
heck if I could tell what it was.

Well I found out soon enough – I
did finally reach the top, and there I
stood like someone struck dumb by
utter astonishment. The massive
building atop the mountain turned out
to be a huge resturant and ski lift, and
there were dozens of ski lifts everywhere,
and snow tractors, and people running

all over the top of the peak and down it – below lay a gigantic resort complex with thousands of people and condo's. To sum it up, I was standing on the less than virgin summit of the famous Squaw Peak, where the Winter Olympics were held. I never have heard of a wilderness boardering on such human multitude. One side of Squaw peak is tranquil, and the other side is a carnival mad house, and there I stood bewildered as I slowly stumbled across the peak, dodging tractors to get down the mountain and out of that area.

So on and on the laughter rang as I danced a fool's game, but understanding rose with it. The world is our mind, and it is our thoughts we attempt to run from, thus there is no escaping humanity wherever you may hide. Even if no people are there, your mind will fill the area with memories of the places and people you ran from. We need find serenity within ourself thru remembrance of our true spiritual reality, then wherever we go, we will find the wilderness and be in the midst of an inner tranquil solitude. To enforce this realization I would go to airports and busy marketplaces and sit in meditation to abide in that center of calm, and thus I found no need to try to outdistance the world, for it is always where one runs to, biting at your heels, for it is your mind you flee. So now I walk tranquil in the wilderness at all times, whether that be the city or virgin lands, and all encounters are welcome; thus the world has stopped chasing me, and I now have the solitude I once sought, and with it the communion I had only dreamed of.

Art Plate 2-13 ~ Sweet Play ~

The stage is set, lines arranged,
curtain rises, we're cast in view,
blinded by light, performance demanded.
Ha! the play,
and the pilgrim a reluctant actor,
seeking refuge behind vague lines,
resting in his sanctuary of doubt.
Spread your wings,
hide in your own reflection,
yet irony will follow,
for the stage is your consciousness,
and the clamoring voices
your own demanding ego;
no where to run,
no secrets to fathom.
We must face ourself,
and sing sweet within the dance,
content in relative play,
just to gain confidence
of truth buried within,
giving the living essence of freedom,
claiming our heritage of strength.
The play be sweet
when realization blooms,
that a stage apart
be of your heart,
and love be your lines,
and oh the drama,
ebb and flow, rising with the tide,
be the blessed communion
the pilgrim sought,
buried before his eyes;
yet vision clears, along with years,
speaks a simple truth,
of spirit whole, and no goal
to burden of the soul;
just a nurturing play,
a sharing of joy,
within an embrace eternal.

Art Plate 2-14 ~ A Spiritual Pilgrim~

We are the perpetual wanderer, traveling a course to recognize ourself. Some must travel deep into physical embrace, others will wander in the quagmire of their mind, and some search the depth of a longing heart. The course be different, yet is the same for all, for any path is a search away from the simplicity of truth. We are that very essence of life called God, and all consciousness is part of this one Reality as aspect of its expression. Those who recognize themself find an incredible joy in the remembrance it brings, and thus they become the dream they wander. They still will sojourn through this land of shadow, for perpetual is the pilgrim's walk, yet their heart will live in the devotion of expressing freedom born of their true nature of spiritual essence. Whether sitting or walking, working or resting, all is meditation within their heart, for this realm which enfolds them provides the avenue of communion which they have created, and it is in this moment that they have accepted the gift of remembrance, and express it in joy as the living consciousness of God.

65

Parable - What am I Lacking?

There was a young man who felt he was not progressing spiritually as fast as he should, so he decided to seek advice from a spiritual warrior. He asked around and finally discovered one who was renowned to have enlightened many people, but his methods were always kept secret.

So he went to the warrior and asked, "I want to live as a monk and become enlightened. Would you please teach me?" The warrior looked at the young man very intently and responded, "I would like to teach you, but I'm afraid there is something that you are lacking. Please meditate on this, and come back when you have fulfilled this lack.

So the young man left a bit discouraged, but was determined to fulfill this need and return, but he didn't know what to do. This made him figure that his lack must be in dedication, for he wasn't very knowledgeable about spiritual practises. So for months he read hundreds of books and practised diligently what he read, till he built up a tremendous confidence of his understanding.

He then went back to the warrior proudly and asked if he could now receive his teachings. But the warrior took one look at him and said, "I'm so sorry, but you still are lacking something. Please go and meditate on this, but do come back as soon as you've discovered your lack.

Reluctantly the young man left and sat alone, puzzled as to what to do. But finally he thought he understood. He had gained knowledge, but didn't put it to any use — he had dedication, but no respect for life, thus he didn't share his knowledge. So he set himself the task of demonstrating his knowledge and shared with all. This brought him great joy, and after several months he felt like a king.

So he went back to the warrior confidently and asked if he could now teach him. The warrior looked at him for quite some time and then said, "you are still lacking something. Please come back as soon as you've realized it."

Greatly discourged the young man dragged himself away. All his friends thought he was wonderful, but this great teacher didn't even feel he was good enough to be a pupil. He was shattered by this defeat, but his spiritual knowledge and the respect he had gained made him try harder to be true to his understanding. So he went about the same tasks as he had been doing, but he no longer looked for praise, for he felt quite inadaquate. The dedication was still there, and he respected all of life, but he had little love for his own spiritual nature. Year after year slowly faded by and he became quite respected by all the town, but he stayed very humble in his knowledge, and slowly he came to love himself and be truly sincere in the humility of his ignorance.

Five years slowly elaped, and one morning he woke with a start and said, "I must go see the warrior." So he visited the warrior and asked, "what am I lacking, tell me, what am I lacking?" The warrior smiled genuinely and replied, "were you ever lacking anything?" The young man bowed and respectfully answered, "thank you for teaching me."

The warrior innocently responded, "did I ever teach you anything?" The young man laughed and said, there are many cunning weasels in the forest, but here on this mountain I've discovered the slyest fox of them all;" at which they both laughed like children.

Comment: What was the young man lacking? He was merely lacking his freedom, and there is no one, or no teaching that can give it to another. We can only inspire others and ourself to become more dedicated and sincere. Knowledge is available for all, and with it we can gain understanding of our true nature. This will foster a respect for life, and thus we make ourself available to share this respect and bring it into a relationship with life. But the hardest lesson to learn is still to come, and that is to realize our ignorance and humbly accept it. This brings true love for ourself, and thus we realize our freedom. Only then can we see that we never really lacked freedom, or could find a method to achieve it. Our freedom is our true Self, and we need only live it as the essence of Ğod that we are.

~ Deep in your heart, beyond the shadows of sight, there is a feeling so very precious; and no one can ever tell you of it, or take it away from you ... ~

~ Meditate on This ~

The mood of a warrior is the subtle art of remembering the miracle of their own existence, and living it as a prayer of the moment. Nothing fancy, just simply sharing love, and dropping everything else that interferes with its expression. No one can place any obligation upon whatever expression of freedom you choose. You are God in form, and your actions are the miracle of life. Let us commune in this truth, and share in oneness the strength of our divine heritage ...

~   ~   ~

We sit in the midst of a miracle, with nothing more to do than observe it. Obligations are self imposed ...

~   ~   ~

Who are you? and where are you? — you are God, experiencing God! Physicality is a dream of your true nature of God — it is a play of consciousness where illusion is its reality. Time and space are vehicles of illusion, and so is your consciousness, for it is your ego sense of separation and forgetfulness. All the play is but shadows, and spiritual realization is the simple remembrance of 'who you are', and 'where you are'. You are God, living the experience of God, through the miracle of life. Remember this and walk blessed within your freedom ...

Journey forward or meditate in peace,
realization of your spiritual essence is
not a pilgrimage. Paths wander amidst a
quagmire of confusing and differing goals,
leading a pilgrim ever onward into hope.
But arrest your doubts, we are built of
truth beyond discovery, blatantly set
before our eyes as the very life and
breath of our consciousness. God be
one whole, and there can be no awareness
separated outside the bounds of God's
expressed reality; even though dream
it may be, we are built of consciousness,
and abide as one totality of awareness.
Thus is the heralding blessing - we
need not look for God, we are God,
and we need but share onto ourself
the divinity brought of individual
awareness, and share this in a
relationship with all life, to foster a
communion within the consciousness
of God. Yet still the road is there,
but now our pilgrimage has intrinsic
value, not a search exterior to projected
goals, but a communion within as
an embrace of our Godhood, and thus
our pilgrimage is a walk of joy,
expressing freedom in the sharing of
our heart. Walk, yes do walk, and
share the gift of a heralding truth.

Wanderings of The Heart

Seven Devils Wilderness ~ August 1987~

The Grand Canyon may be the epitome of grandeur, and Yosemite rings forth of awe inspiring splendeur, but the canyon carved deepest into the western earth lies at the base of Seven Devils wilderness. As I stood atop He-Devil peak, with such outlandish peaks surrounding me like 'She-Devil', 'The Ogre', 'Twin Imps', 'Devil's Tooth', 'The Goblin', 'Devil's Throne' and 'The tower of Babel', I had a panorama stretching not only to all horizons, but downward some 8,000 feet to the raging Snake River below. What a tremendous slice thru these rugged mountains the Snake River has cut. My view stretched to the Eagle Cap wilderness, where just a month earlier I stood atop its peaks gazing with longing to where I now stood. To the east lies 3 million acres of 'The River of No Return Wilderness', which I had just been blessed to explore. What a grand spot I stood upon within these sacred Indian mountains, and below me by several thousand feet lay a rock basin filled with azure lakes, which sent bubbling flows of crystaline water plummeting down the cliffs to the Snake River below.

I had wound my way thru a series of passes and across the flank of the Tower of Babel in hope of descent to Sheep lake; and then my eyes looked straight up at the towering He-Devil peak rising to 9,393 feet, and I knew I must stand atop its powerful presence.

The effort brought a deepening communion with this range of rock, and as I stood upon the crest I was awestruck by the incredible power the Grand Tetons have issued forth in sending the Snake River to carve such an incredible spectacle. My journey down brought me cross country around the Devil's Tooth, but shortly after I was to witness a blessed event.

Traversing along the ridge I came to an area rarely traveled, and here the cliff dropped several thousand feet below this knife like escarpment. The colors and formations incrusted into the cliffs rock drew my interest, but suddenly my attention was startled by a loud noise coming from the middle area of the jagged cliffs. I surveyed the rock face diligently, and oh how blessed I was to see four mountain goats climbing their way up the sheer cliff. They were about a half mile to my left and at least 1000 feet below me, about mid way in the nearly vertical cliff. Mountain goats are incredible, they can climb nearly any surface, and as I watched, three of the goats slowly made their way up one vertical face after another. It was just spellbinding to watch them, and I was sure that they would get stuck somewhere, but within a half hour three of them had climbed over 1000 feet to the crest above.

The fourth mountain goat had seemed to change his mind, for when he had ascended half way up the cliff he then turned around and made an angled descent toward my direction. My eyes were focused on his movements, for now he had crossed the base of the cliff and was once again beginning to climb

73

just below me. I had to climb along the cliff and lean over its edge, but I managed to keep him in view till he was about 500 feet directly below me. But then he went out of my sight, and at the same time it began to softly rain, so I decided to crouch under the small pine tree next to me on the edge of the cliff. I figured it would stop raining soon and I could once again take up the hunt to find where my mountain goat departed to.

But a search proved unnecessary, for to my amazed delight, the mountain goat all of a sudden popped over the edge of the vertical cliff; and there he stood towering in all his magnificence, looking back over the cliff he had just ascended. He stood only 15 feet away, and the rain turned out to be a great blessing, for he didn't see me as I crouched under my little pine tree. He surveyed his domain with majestic turns of his head, as he stood on the very brink of the 2,000 foot cliff. His long flowing hair was pure white, and stretched at least a foot. But what surprised me was his size, for as I watched him from far above he looked so small, but now as I sat only 15 feet away I could appreciate his towering form of at least 200 pounds.

After 15 minutes of majestically posing above his realm, he walked along the cliff away from my spot to an area where a finger of rock jutted out into space, and there he leaped to a secluded spot where the rain did not fall. I at once crawled on hands and knees to the rock just above him, and there & lay with my eyes peeping over, quietly watching the regal king sit within his private throne. For an hour & watched till light was dimming and home was issuing a beckoning call. How blessed to have this rare opportunity of heart communion, and so reluctantly & bid the king my fond farewell.

The ridge brought me back to my home nestled in the trees, and dinner brought on a mood of reverie, as & sincerely offered my gratitude for the grace which so abundantly flowed that day. Just the day before & had stood at the edge of a shallow pond watching an enormous bull moose dip his magnificent antlers into the water and bring up the succulent grasses. And at Eagle Cap & stood atop the peak and watched a herd of well over 100 elk bugle as they raced across the sloping medow below. Deer surround me in abundance, and eagles dot the sky — salmon leap in joy, and the songs of birds provide me with eternal music. Oh how blessed & am to stand in the midst of a living consciousness, which has adopted an infinite variety of ways to express its joy of divinity. Those who sit behind walls will never understand this joy so exhuberant in creation's relationship. One must be within the living presence of life's explosion, and feel the power and wonder of its call, and only then can one look at life and know in their heart that all existence is one reality of equal essence — realization is an experience, for we are God, living the experience of God...

Art Plate 2~16 ~ A Simple Gift ~

A simple man I met on the street,
his face had lines of laughter,
and so contagious was his smile,
that my heart soared just to see him.
Possessions were not of his wealth,
yet treasures greater than kings,
were held sacred within his heart,
and cast as seed to the wind.
Mother showers a tranquil peace,
the grace of quenching rain,
to slack the thirst of his eyes,
and bring freedom to his vision.
Joy exudes as his gift,
to nurture of his soul,
bestowing this simple offering as rain,
to a land parched and barren plain.
He walks in a shadowed dream,
more real than the pain,
and few understand his simple smile,
yet freedom cannot be explained.
His day is a walk,
no different than yours,
his road a weaving course,
that carries him beyond,
our stage and path, and force.
So now he holds aloft a key,
to share a secret plain,
that precious time be abundantly there,
if words of inner joy will share
the gift of your smile.

Life is outrageous, and how you interpret it determines your level of consciousness. Though all is one in essence, everything has its arena of awareness in which to order its individual expression. At what level do you view this man? What does his outrageous posture speak to your mind and heart? Is he trying to show that everything points above to God? Is he demonstrating that he has renounced the world and now stands empty handed? Or perhaps he is being robbed! Does your mind see him as a spiritual pilgrim or a fool? In the world use your mind to establish a relationship of mutual understanding, but in communion with life and spirit, let your heart direct your vision. See and feel the spiritual nature within, and let this inner sight dictate your level of consciousness. You cannot gain wisdom from a dedicated spiritual soul if you view his life with the reasoning of the mind, but the love within your heart can grasp the purpose of their sincere commitment to spiritual communion, and imbue the value of their heart realization. We live in a miracle, and spiritual sight is upside down and backwards to the mind's vision, so be alert to the outrageousness of this spiritual miracle of life, and laugh in the joy it demonstrates in life's absurd and wondrous play.

78

Parable ~ The Barbarians

There once lived a very devout monk in a country well know for its spiritual zeal. The people of the country were very civilized, and spent the day conversing of religious matters. How joyous the monk was to be in the temple observing his rituals and talking with the other monks.

But one day the bad news came; the senior abbot told the monk that because he was so dedicated, he was going to be sent to a barbaric land to help civilize the people into religion. The monk was appalled, but being obedient he consented to go and do his best.

After a long journey he arrived in a country he never heard of, and was shown to a small hut where he was to live. He was so terrified of these barbaric people that for several days he didn't even leave the hut. But eventually he rounded up his courage, and decided to speak to the people. So out into the village he went and introduced himself to many of the people, and attempted to speak of religious matters, but true enough the barbaric people would not speak of any of the spiritual subjects the monk brought up, but would just continue about their work. The monk was so discouraged, there was no one to converse with or who cared about religion, it made him so sad he cried. But he did see that the people offered him no harm, and in fact were very curteous to him, and seemed to be honest people who worked hard and had respect for their land, and seemed sincere in their ways and humble in their life. So at least the monk felt he was living in a land he could tolerate, but he felt such compassion for the religiously deprived barbarians.

After months of trying to get thru to these spiritally deficient people, the monk began to pray earnestly for a way to bring understanding to them. His compassion rose to such an extent, that he cried openly for God to give him the wisdom necessary to bring realization to this land of barbarians.

That night the monk had a dream, and in it he was told by a venerable, old priest that the monk had misjudged the spirituality of the barbarians. The priest explained that for ones who have gone beyond intellectual premise and live true to their heart, that religious dialogue is unnecessary, and that the mundane activities of life are their prayer. The barbarians church was in the respect for the land they loved, and their spiritual talk was the sincerity of their actions, and this brought them humility. The priest then said that people who preached religious truths all day were possibly ones who were trying to convince themselves of these truths; and if they had to surround themselves with reminders of the truth, and spoke only to ones who would agree with their opinions then they often were weak in faith. The priest ended by saying that the practise of religious faith is a high step on the ladder towards realization of truth; but there is a step beyond it, and that is to be the truth and stop trying to convince yourself of the truth — just to simply be, and live true to yourself.

The monk then woke up and sat dazed in his bed — could what the priest just said be the truth? Was he really the barbarian and the people in the village really the civilized ones? Was the country he left full of barbarians who were not totally convinced of the truth, so they had to repeat it and worship it to try to establish it? And were these people so convinced that they didn't need to discuss what was so obvious to them; were they already living the truth of their Self?

So the monk went out and was going to ask all these questions, but realized that this would only be talking religious speculation. So he went to one of the farmers and asked, "could I please help you in the field today?" The farmer was genuinely pleased, and said he would be honored if the monk would be gracious enough to help. All that day they worked in silence and never spoke of any religious concepts, and yet at the end of the day the monk felt full of strength and joy. The farmer and monk spoke words of thanks in the humility of brotherly sharing, and then departed. The monk now looked at everyone in the village in a new light of understanding, for he had never realized before that day that everyone there was happy. They were simple in their ways and had a great love for life, enough love not to interfere with the monk and tell him that he still had alot to learn of spiritual expression; in their wisdom they allowed him time to grow and accept, as his capacity would allow.

Parable ~ Dirt is not Outside

There was a small boy who loved to play in the dirt, and at the end of the day he was always quite a mess. His mother would scold him daily while washing him, "why do you get so filthy;" but the boy didn't feel dirty. As the boy grew older he associated with all the neighborhood boys, and some were known to be hoodlums. His mother would scold him, "don't be seen with such filth;" but the boy didn't feel dirty when he talked to them. Then one day the boy told a lie, and no matter how much he washed, he always felt dirty from that day on.

Comment: We are the world, both body and mind. Physical association with nature or those expressing ignorance will not bring impurity into our manifest form, for all this universe is equal in its physical nature. But to speak an untruth and embody the lie, brings an impurity into our consciousness that cannot be cleansed. They are embodied into your mind, and no petition of prayer will remove a lie from your life. A person doesn't have to understand any subtle spiritual laws to know if they speak honestly, or if they are a liar unto their words. You cannot run from yourself, and to 'be true to yourself' is the highest law of this universe; it is the foundation of all spiritual life, and the only door available for evolving into higher planes of awareness.
    Be true, speak true, live true, and thus you will be the truth...

83

Art Plate 2-18 ~ Prayer of Life ~

Life is a prayer, and our outer actions and appearance must reflect the sincere devotion within. The truth of our life must be felt as a vibrant pulse which dictates the priority of spiritual communion, and the strength this builds must be shared as an expression of devotion with all life. Thus all activities are the prayer of communion, and one no longer needs special activities to demonstrate their realization, but can express it in every circumstance of life's unfoldment. Moment by moment their prayer blossoms as they unceasingly live the remembrance of their communion. They are that essence of God manifested into the breath of life, and each moment is the wondrous opportunity to share this miracle of being the experience of God. Respect of the truth, and humility in their effort, bring true sincerity of demonstration, and joyous communion is the grace of their prayer. How wondrous it is to feel the presence of Mother as the very prayer of your life ...

85

Art Plate 2-19 ~ Sincerity of Devotion ~

Spiritual expression is personal. It does not matter how you express your devotion, as long as it sincerely mirrors your heart, for physical name and form are not the reality, but only reflect concepts of limitation. How you choose to honor the reality of your soul is an individual offering of prayer; it is the total prayer of all your life, and includes every activity you engage your consciousness in. Sincerity is the only common spiritual practice, and from it spring the unlimited forms of its devotion. They are all basicly equal, as is all physical expression, it is the awareness of the individual within his activity that provides for distinction. There is no one truth, there are only varying perspectives fostered by sincerity of conviction, and from this platform we offer our heart in recognition of the truth within us. Thus truth becomes remembrance of our reality of being, and an honoring to its divine expression of consciousness, but the heart must be free to determine its unique way of sincerity. The way you chose expresses the consciousness of God, and you are the life of God's devotion.

Fragrance of Love

Oh my sister so lovely,
picking flowers to offer
upon your altar of devotion.
But wait,
your basket is full,
and I have not yet
seen you smell the fragrance
of the beauty you hold.
You rush outside
to rape the splendor
of the plant's tender love,
and then quickly indoors
you return with its bounty,
to offer it to your deity.
But it is your own surrender you offer,
and the blossom you clasp
so dearly in your hand
is but ornament
to your prayerful duty.
Their life has been surrendered
to your ideal of worship,
and all they have offered
has been set aside with their breath.
Is your prayer more precious
then the life of their dreams?
Is it asking too much
to pay affection
to the one you maim,
as an offering
to your own life?
If your devotion to God be true,
then life itself is the grandest prayer.
Honor your object of worship,
and pluck its life with respect—
inhale the fragrance
of its dying breath
as an honoring of its sacrifice.

Thus walk to your altar
in honor and respect,
laying down the offering you've brought,
as the surrender of life
to the God you both are;
for the flower is your very essence,
and in humility
recognize your equality.
Then you've caused no injury,
but have willingly offered up your life
to the God within you,
as you kneel in prayer
within the altar of love;
and the fragrance
will fill the temple with purity,
as the truth of devotion
from the guileless heart of a child.

Art Plate 2-20 ~ Fragrance of Love

Wanderings of The Heart

Lizard head Wilderness ~ Aug. 1986 ~

What a magnificent land Colorado is for those souls like myself who find such tremendous joy standing atop the craggy mountain escarpments, breathing that rarified air of adventure and challenge, and gazing below on the vast panorama of life's more explored terrain. There is an elevated consciousness as well as a strengthened physical body when climbing the rocky flanks of these serene titans of living bone. The communion is one of direct contact, and not of intellectual premise, and all the nonsense of worldly speculation is reduced to ashes when the mountain puts its demands upon your integrity, for there is a price to pay to stand atop the crest of these mighty giants of granite. It is the payment of your selfhood, for one must relinquish their pride and stand in humility, respect and gratitude if they hope to receive the blessings that Mother Earth bestows when standing upon her pure upper reaches.

Delorus Peak rises as a towering cone that provides an outstanding panorama of the Mt. Wilson range. It is 13,290 feet of dense elk laden forest rising into a talus escarpment, surrounded by peaks of great stature. My climb thru the forest was slowed by the sight of grazing elk and the abundance of fragrant mountain flowerings, all glistening with morning dew. But soon enough I broke out of the trees and the incline increased till I finally was using my hands to scramble up the jagged talus slope. For several thousand feet the loose rock provided a tedious effort, but great weather blessed the day with a cool, clear sky. When my arrival did finally occur I was treated to an outstanding, vast vista of granite needle peaks rising out of the backbone of the Rockies, surrounded by lush green valleys all florescent in autumn's coat and dotted with emerald lakes, and beautiful cloud patterns filled the sky with unearthly forms of splendeur.

Hours passed in slow reverie of the awesome display of nature's wonders, and provided a tranquil communion that the Earth graciously bestow on those not asking of its gifts. My lunch of fruit had been devoured with great appreciation, and my meditative nap refreshed both spirit and body, so now it was time for a loving farewell and a descent down the steep ravine that led to the valley below. The creek I followed increased its size as it bubbled and cascaded rapidly, forming one gorgeous waterfall after another, with lush moss, ferns and wildflowers filling every crevice and blanketing both sides of the ravine. Eventually the ravine formed into the valley and I was once again treading a course thru the virgin forest, engulfed by beautiful meadows dotted with ponds, and crystal, cold streams winding there course thru dense stands of pines and furs. The elk ran off thru flowering fields of flashing color, as the birds gently serenaded my quiet footsteps.

The next day found me proceeding westward along the ridge, and climbing the next giant of granite in my path, but it brings back no significant memory. But that is not the case for the following peak I climbed on that isolated ridge, for my next ascent was of the world renowned Groundhog Peak. Well perhaps Groundhog peak is virtually unknown, and its height is only in the 12,000 foot range, and it is surrounded by absolutely spectacular peaks (like Lone Peak which I attempted after Groundhog), but I had a truly unforgetable experience atop Groundhog peak that will forever endear its twisted rock to my heart.

Groundhog peak is volcanic rock instead of granite, and doesn't have the picturesque shape or awesome appearance that does its neighbors, but it is unexpectedly taller than it first appears and the terrain of the ridge is strikingly beautiful in its desolate colors, and the view from the top is nearly as fine as the other peaks. One major difficulty in reaching its crest is that the last few hundred feet of ascent is on the most loosely placed volcanic rock I've ever seen. The steepness of that last little push combined with the loose rock made it as trying to climb a moving avalanche of razor blades - keen attention is needed if one wants to walk away from Groundhog unscathed. But there was even a greater drawback to Groundhog, for after all the hard work to reach its crest, I found that it came right to a pinpoint top, and

I didn't even have a place to sit down and relax after all my effort.

I normally do not alter the top of any peak out of respect for the virgin quality of its sacred reaches, but darn if this Groundhog peak didn't need someone to do something about its total lack of hospitality to worn out trekers. I stood there bewildered for a few moments looking at the utter bareness of its needle point, and then I said to myself, 'well I'm just going to have to do something about this situation', and I put down my pack and set about the task of rebuilding the entire top of Groundhog peak. I didn't intend at first to do such a major revamp of the summit, I was only going to move a couple of rocks so I could sit down, but something seemed to possess me when I pulled out my leather gloves and rolled up my sleeves.

As I started to move rock around I noticed that my efforts would all be in vain because there was no substantial foundation on which to build. Groundhog has a 500 foot straight drop of craggy rock on one side, and 300 feet of steeply sloping volcanic talus rising to a point on the other side. What I needed was a platform, so the first thing I had to do was to reshape the rock about 5-10 feet below the top to be stable, and add rock to the edges for support. Sounds real easy writing about it; well the actuality of it was that I had to climb down the 500 foot rock face and hang from extremely loose rock with one hand while I pushed rocks into the crevices with the other

93

94

hand, to make the top lying rock more stable. Yes I know it sounds crazy, and as a matter of fact it was crazy. The sloping talus side was really no easier, for I had to move quite large, jagged boulders to build a flat area. While I was at it I built nice steps at the top area and a front alcove before the highest platform. Now I set about building a small shelter on the top, sort of a rounded half colosseum with windows, ledges and an opening for a door; and of course I erected a large pillar signifying its entrance, sort of crowning the colosseum like a glorious mast of a ship. Below this main structure I built steps leading down four feet to a lower platform where I could lay down, and lined the stairs with a wall and windows. The colosseum was perfect in shape but dull in color, being mostly gray volcanic rock, so once again I hung over the 500 foot cliff and grabbed the most beautiful licken covered flat rocks, and lined the inside of the colosseum with beauty greater than the paintings of a medieval church.

Four hours had elapsed and I had not even looked at the view, but now atop Groundhog peak was a castle built of love, and with respect I only can hope it was to the honor of its humble nature of power. So finally I sat in the colosseum and communed with the peace that reigned after my endeavor, but unfortunately I had expended all the time that I would have had to sit in meditation; so I dedicated my efforts to those who would come later to Groundhog's crest, and bade my farewell as I sent my love to the miracle and mysteries this realm so graciously offers, then ever so shakily made my way down Groundhog's loose, treacherous talus.

My attempt to restructure the top of Groundhog peak was one of extreme danger, but life is equal in its expression and no one activity has any greater importance or relevance than another. To die in some totally meaningless task is no less a death than to die while engaged in a heroic endeavor, for our body is of the earth and will fall back into the elements of the Earth's body, and the only criterion that makes a life worthwhile is the challenge that the person has accepted. We come into life to experience its moment of unfoldment, and it is an ego of selfhood that determines a relative value, when in fact all is equal in its scope as the miracle of existence, and expression only indicates the integrity of individual consciousness. Equality bears the responsibility of sincerity of intent, for only thru respect, humility and love can a relative world bear value and give a direction of purpose. To live in freedom is our purpose, and all life must be the expression of this challenge of freedom, thus all endeavors have value in equality whether ridiculous in nature or encompassing in scope. As long as one lets their heart soar in freedom in all activities of life, then death will be your friend and never catch you unprepared.

Parable - The Mountain Summit

A zen master and his disciple decided to climb the highest peak in that area, a spot renowned for its spectacular view. Off they went up its rocky flank, but the going was very tough. Hour after hour they labored till finally the summit lay in view. But as they neared the crest, the clouds dropped down and covered them in a thick fog. When they reached the top they could barely see in front of them, and their long awaited view was not to be found.

The master was smiling radiantly, but the disciple was very annoyed and spoke out, "why are you so happy, after all this work we aren't going to be able to see anything." The master replied, "the fog on this mountain is the same as the world. We never see our true nature because it lies hidden by the fog of worldly desires and attachments. And here we don't see the true reality surrounding us beause it is hidden by the fog of our attempted achievement. We are in the fog of illusion, and if we but sit and meditate on the reality of our true nature, then the fog of illusion will lift and we will see the truth; thus they both sat in meditation. After an hour the master told the disciple to open his eyes to reality, and as he did he beheld the most beautiful panorama imaginable, for the clouds had lifted and the magnificent land stretched in wondrous expanse.

From that day on the disciple no longer let the fog of worldly activity and the clouds of his own desire obscure the truth of reality that lay hidden, yet beyond them.

Art Plate 2-22 ~ Sincerity's Joy ~

Spiritual realization is effervescent, and its enthusiasm is the link that brings communion into physical expression; and this exuberance is just a natural flow when sincerity blooms in devotion as the prayer of life. Spiritual sincerity is the joy of remembrance, not a superficial emotion, but a vibrant communion of the heart giving purpose to life's prayer, and freedom to our soul. Joy, blissful joy, to remember your spirit eternal; ah but here a word of vigilance, for the pilgrim must be on guard for seriousness. Sincerity is our freedom, it is truth in demonstration, but seriousness is just a fool's game that burdens the heart with the ignorance of a demanding selfhood, and helps foster further forgetfulness. Sincerity is the platform that wisdom resides upon, but anyone who takes life seriously has forgotten their true self, and the best they can ever attain is knowledge of the relative. Joy is embodied when one communes with life directly, and receives in respectful humility the boundless blessings this universe freely bestows. Sincerity is the key to this door of wonder, but seriousness is most definitely a brick wall that enforces an ego of conceptual separateness. Laugh in this dance of life's unfoldment, you are under no burden. We are the freedom of God within the consciousness of manifest form, and to live in this sincerity bestows the blessing of life's ultimate gift, and that is Joy...

A pilgrim walks not by strength,
but by the grace of Mother.
Who can speak of joy
comparable to Mother's gift,
of blessed communion
thru the heart,
embraced divine in tender love.
Deeper than life
bridges this bond,
eternity its sacred home,
and here a pilgrim
bows in reverence,
enfolded of the gracious dream;
Mother breathing his very life,
and truth a gate back home;
but why not wander here awhile
tasting bliss divine,
and sharing the joy unbridled.
Time is precious,
and Mother eternal,
and the play a devoted path,
to pour love upon the fire,
sacred the light it burns.
And oh the joy,
the exuberant joy,
to inhale life into a heart
beating the rhythm
of Mother's dance,
and & a singer
to please her purity,
chanting in love divine,
offering my prayers,
blessed by my tears,
to the purging fire,
which burns eternal
as our soul...

Freedom's Gentle Knock

Ever so early this morning
I came a knocking,
to sound the call of freedom,
lest you slumber away in forgetfulness.
Three times I attempted
entrance to your door,
but deep in sleep,
you gave no answer
to my silent beckoning summons.
The sky is filled with purples and reds,
from the radiance of the heralding sun,
but a dream has carried you
beyond this realm, oblivious to my plea.
Awake! Awake!
This time is so very precious,
fleeting away with the clouds,
lost into the labyrinth
of a wandering mind.
I am here to issue
the call of remembrance,
for time cannot be recaptured,
and no one can return
colors sublime of a rising sun,
as you idly dream tales
of the future gone by.
The blessings of the moment
plead for your heart,
with no desire to imprison you,
but your spirit answers not
the call so sweet,
and freedom now sadly leaves
to knock upon another door.
One last glance over the shoulder,
one last faint knock upon a door locked.
But the colors of a brilliant awakening
have faded from hope,
and now only harsh light
remains to blind the mind,

no different than the darkness
of a closed heart.
Each day freedom returns
as the first light of a beckoning hope,
to sound the herald eternal
of challenge born anew.
But it is we who must answer the call,
for no one can remove our slumber;
it is we who must rake the mind
and dispell the dream,
and run to answer the knock so sweet,
leaving all behind for that rare glimpse
of freedom's radiant hues.
All of eternity freedom has waited
in the patience of a love divine;
and can a dream ever compare
with the reality of a miracle.
Slowly freedom retreats as he hears
the clamoring of a wakening mind,
for he has come to share the wonder
with the innocence of a pure heart.
One day your soul will yearn
for the soft footsteps
of freedom's tender approach.
No knock will be necessary,
for your heart will leap to the door,
gently following in the wake
of freedom's cutting edge.
Your ears must be keenly tuned
to the sound of freedom's call,
and remembrance must be
the only longing of your heart,
for freedom will never clamor at your door,
demanding of your communion.
It is you who must be ready
to respectfully walk
in the humility of your sincerity,
for only when your heart be pure
will freedom's feet stir your soul.
Oh the joy to taste the miracle,
and walk this land as freedom's wonder...

Wandering of The Heart

The Desert's Touch ~ Moonshine Wash ~ Sept. 88~

Fiery red, the burning globe
brought life to the desert floor.
Basking in its florescent hues,
it fed my soul
with the energy needed to awaken.
One by one the sandstone pillars
lit into hues of brilliance,
forming concealing shadows
on the desert sands,
as each bush now lit
into flames of radiant light.
No equal has the desert
for that explosive glow
of dawn's fiery touch,
and I could do no more
than bask in its glory,
as my heart burned
with its heralding call.
Hours waned away in morning reverie,
but now the canyons
beckoned of a Siren's call,
and my feet stirred
to follow their echo.
Down into the twisted arroyo,
jagged with sagebrush,
ever winding deeper
into the Earth's swallowing abyss.
Sinking into dark recesses
of convoluted sandstone,
the sheer walls rose within me
a fearful twinge of expectation.
The canyon ever deepened,
narrowing into a thin slot,
allowing but a glancing step
upon its fluted walls.

Deep and cold, pools awaited,
and I stemmed their depths.
Traversing drop offs
of ever increasing complexity,
I ventured to wonder
if this thin crack in the rock
would ever lead its constricting walls
out of this claustrophobic maze.
But at last a widening turn,
and now appears a hidden cleft
buried within this labyrinth
of tortured rock.
The raging sun now released,
baked me in the brilliancy
of searing white light,
and I sought the shadows
to hold firm the thread
of my fragile life.
The black stained, red rock
radiated waves of intense heat,
and my water containers soon emptied
down my parched throat
in grateful appreciation
of its life giving force.
No wind to sooth my brow,
as sweat dripped slowly down my face,
but fruit eased the pangs of hunger,
and a nap brought living energy
to this physical vehicle of my spirit.
The barren desert appears lifeless,
yet within its twisted canyon recesses
there truly blooms forth
the radiant touch of life's song.
Brushes fragrant with bloom
line the shaded walls;
flowers bravely shot upward
from the harsh gravel bottom;
springs flowed forth from crevices
etched in the enormous rock walls.

Ah, how the touch of liquid life
brings the desert fauna
to its silent beckoning.
Hours and life wore on,
and the cocoon of red stained walls
brought a sublime tranquility,
for all sound was absorbed
into this omnipotent structure of stone.
Life would have me bask
in the power of its presence,
but hours have no function here,
and reasons only deafly count
the layers of mud upon the walls.
Though the canyon issues
no beckoning lure,
to make its stark beauty my home,
I respectfully say with humility
that it nurtures my soul
and inspires my heart;
and one day soon
I shall traverse its depth
to partake of its rare food,
of blessings given thru communion,
and truth silently spoken
in simplicity of spiritual renewal.

Art Plate 2-24 ~ Enfolded ~

Fool I Am

I came to discover
the secrets of the ages,
and behold,
each blade of grass,
every struggling weed,
every bird in song
would dearly love to teach me;
yet I am still a fool
in ignorance of their truths.
How joyously life spreads before me,
showing the mystery of my soul;
yet I am wrapped
in a blanket of delusion,
looking no further
than my own self awareness,
content in my fond forgetfulness.

So here I wander
a merry path to nowhere,
while every rock and tree
tries desperately
to keep me from falling
on my face.
How compassionate they are
to let me dwell in ignorance,
while I sing and dance
amidst their love.

Art Plate 2-25 ~ Life of One Soul

Have you taken life without remorse?
Oh how the wings glisten iridescent,
transparent beauty of blinding speed,
and so beneficently
they cool our heated brow
with a ferocious beat.
We look for death,
the burgeons of destruction,
killing our very self in confusion,
sacrificing communion in haste
to brush away life from our soul.
Look at those wings born of beauty,
see the life linked to your own,
and perhaps a kind word will suffice,
as the world persistently encroaches,
for the task of vigilance
is also persistent,
in giving, and giving of love...

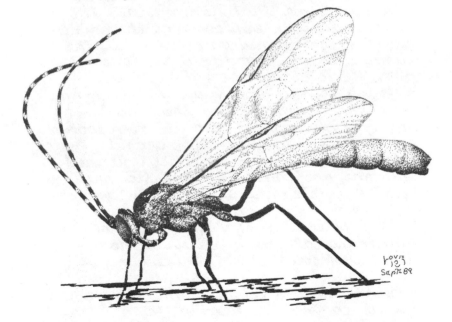

Wanderings of The Heart

Valley of The Gods, Utah ~ Oct. 1988 ~

Twenty miles of hard hiking graced my eyes with a night of gentle slumber, but the morning called to my heart 'Awake, you fool, Awake'. I opened my eyes to the outrageous colors of an incredible sunrise - it was astonishing! The sky was lit in miriad tones of deep orange and gold, and thousands of puffy clouds were totally ablaze with color of every hue imaginable. Quickly I ran outside to find a clear spot to view this glorious array of splendor, but I was in a pinyon-juniper flat, and nowhere could I find a clear view of the impending sunrise. I ran all around and finally found a satisfactory place, but I lost much precious time that had marked the most beautiful explosion of changing light. I communed in silence, till the sun's brilliance made it no longer possible to stare upon its glory.

Back to my van I went, but upon reaching home, I stood there realizing my foolishness. I ran all over looking for an area to view this grand sunrise, when I could have so easily stepped onto my roof and had a perfect viewing spot. I berated myself for my ignorance, but then the lesson struck me.

The perception of light from the sun's heralding call, with all its wondrous display of color, was the blessing of a gift. And as a gift, perception can be observed in a fleeting moment of miracle, but it cannot be held, or even longed for – it is just present, and if we are in the moment there can be communion within our Self. This is life – the gift is present and we have the wondrous opportunity to commune with the mystery of our being.

    I missed the splendor of sunrise's color, as nature beckoned to a drowsy head, but still I lost nothing, only an opportunity to commune to greater depths. It is a travesty to sleep away the blessing of life, and this is the warrior's relentless vigil, to grasp each opportunity of communion and embrace it with their heart, but there is no victory or defeat involved if the moment of opportunity is lost. We are the essence of reality, and life is presented as avenue of awareness, and whatever we perceive within this play of consciousness is but the blessing to experience the Self of our Godhood. All perception within manifestation is experienced in completeness as the totality of our joint essence of life. I can not experience all of manifest's wonder, but since I am one with all existence, then I am the one perceiver, and all of perception is but my shadow. Perception mirrors forth awareness expressed of Reality, and we are an essence of a dream of consciousness in free expression. Thus each moment of opportunity fulfills itself, and we can do no more than to live in the respect and graciousness of this gift.

Parable ~ The Wealthy Beggers

Their was a simple man who lived deep in the forest in a little hut. He had few possessions, but his home was his kingdom, for he felt like a king surrounded by the wonders of nature. Each day he would walk amidst its beauty, drinking from the golden chalices of buttercups, and walking on the finest tapestries of lush green moss. His mind was serene and his heart content, so how could he desire the lifeless objects of the world, when he had the live, vibrant reality of nature as his treasuretrove.

One day he was helping a man who was quite wealthy, and along came the man's son trying to manage with many cumbersome items; so the simple man stopped the boy and gave him his knapsack, to help make his load easier to manage. The father just shook his head in sympathy, for he felt sorry that the man had so little, and now gave even that away. But the man had great compassion for these poor, wealthy people, for they were as beggars in life. They had spent their precious gift of life accumulating objects of trivial use, thus they had never established contact with the beauty that enfolded them. They had forfeited the communion of life, and lost their precious, irretrievable time as well, just to collect objects of temporary convienence. They were chained to the ignorance of social concepts, thus saw no miracles in life. Oh how the man wished he could give them the fragrance of the flowers, or the beauty of the moon, but in their greed they had lost the capacity to accept such wondrous gifts.

You Need Not Ask

I ask for nothing,
yet blossoms flower forth
to bath me in fragrance.

I ask for nothing,
yet nurturing rains gently descend
to slack my yearning thirst.

I ask for nothing,
yet the sun sustains me in warmth,
as it radiantly lights my way.

Dare I ask for enlightenment
in a realm that has no lack.
Softly the wind speaks
of wisdom beyond consciousness,
yet if I were to seek it
I'd be thousands of miles away.
Everything is provisioned for
in this outrageous journey of life,
and to ask for sustenance,
only shows
that understanding is what I lack.

I ask for nothing,
yet everything
I have received.

Wanderings of The Heart

Tribute To a Desert Storm ~ Sept. 89~

This day was captured in fury.
Massive billows of black hung ominous,
heralding the apprehension
wrought of a desert storm.
The twisted rock of Utah,
gashed deep with canyons
thru massive reefs of stone,
seldom feel the life
brought of a quenching rain.
It is a parched land of stark beauty,
and the storm approaches
with a rare magnificence of its own.
Tho' the sun still brightly glares,
the wind now forcasts its presence,
as the tempest roars its call,
with red sand flying in swirls;
stout bushes bend in submission,
and my van rocks,
just a toy cast on an angry sea.
Now the distant horizon slowly fades,
as a sheet of water steadily approaches.
Isolated thunderheads build
as monolithic sculptures,
rising higher, ever higher,
cast in creams and whites above,
but black as ebony below.
And from this canopy strikes ominous,
as lightening flashes a warning threat.
Thunder peals thru the canyons,
echos reverberating louder and louder,
silencing the banshee wail of the wind,
or is it they are both in comradery
to raise the dead from ancient slumber.
FLASHing in explosive fury,
I gaze in sheer amazement —
and then the rain.

What vengeance it blasts,
like rocks hurled from the stars,
adding an ever increasing voice
to nature's wail of power.
But oh how subtle Mother can be,
for now a stupendous double rainbow
graces the sky directly above,
but with a touch of irony,
as lightening flashes within its arms,
giving the prismatic colors
an added highlight of brilliance;
growing in intensity,
it casts its spectrum of light
across the blackened storm canopy,
and ever so slowly,
moves as the final crescendo
to the dying rays
of an awesome epitaph.
But the desert holds a vast repertoire,
and surprise is its laughter.
The winds subsided, the storm halted,
and night approached in secretive crawl;
so off into the horizon I walked,
as the lightening flashed rapid.
The sky entire
lit with each blast of brilliance,
sending bolts thru a shattered sky.
Dying colors from a forlorn sun
lit the highest crests
of the massive, fluffy billows,
as lightening silhouetted
the blackened mass,
in stark white of surrealistic shadows.
Incredible - just unfathomable -
what grandeur is the scale of this drama,
while stars poke their nosey presence
inbetween cracks of shattered clouds,
and intruding colors of reds and purples
tried to steal the glory of lightening's call;
but ah to me, the observer of the show,
no play could be more sublime.

I walked, and walked,
into the lightening's embrace,
but scattered drops issued a warning call.
Ha, I turned and yet another cloud
was sneaking into the show,
and so entrapped me into its vengeance.
But Mother is kind to those of innocence,
for though rain splattered,
it exspent no fury upon my head,
just a cool refreshment
to Utah's warm night air.
Hours did pass as I watched breathlessly,
and on the show flashed.
Sitting in wonder,
respectful of magnificence,
and awed by the power,
I drifted to sleep
in the arms of the lull;
but awoke to stars
filling a cloud splattered sky,
and curious the east horizon was brightening.
But no sun would dare at this hour,
so yes, it was the moon in glory,
bringing a silvery touch
to the edges of each billowy form.
The clouds lay quietly still
as the moon rose in heralding light,
first orange then gold,
but colors do deceive,
and as it made its wayward climb,
thru thin layers of stationary whiteness,
its color did trick the eye,
now yellow, then paler, then white,
and lit the sky in defiance
to the lightening's dying gasps.
Hours more I watched;
sleep is always available,
but the Earth is glorious explosion
is a Siren's call to my heart,
so on I watched,
and let the grandeur soak my heart

in its life giving beauty.
But my eyes called out their plot,
and lowered to my heart's dismay,
but awoke as darkness
still captured the sky.
Stars and moon lay in still silence,
untouchable yet so near,
and now the east
once again pales into lightness.
The sun in overpowering glory
now demands the stage,
and so it rose,
thru the ages of destiny,
and the spent storm clouds
lit in spectrums of brilliance
that brought awe to mind and voice.
All thirst of the eye
could easily be filled,
within this panorama
stretching to the horizon,
and out into the ether —
fields of gold, drifting in red sand;
gnarled junipers in statuesque relief;
twisted slabs of rock in fiery red;
monolithic mountain escarpments
reaching as fingers to the heavens;
a silvery moon in a purple-blue sky;
clouds of prisma beauty
filling the horizon;
and ah but yes, a golden globe
overwhelming all with its presence.
I sit amazed at the beauty,
and in respect acknowledge its power.
I am one with its grandeur,
for consciousness needs a reflection
to observe its glory;
and thus I walk
as the prayer of life,
and in humility
I watch, I watch . . .

Art Plate 2-26 ~ Honoring Life ~

I raise my arms
to honor life,
and accept the mystery
that clouds my vision.
I am embraced of spirit,
and seek the grace
of eternal communion.
I honor life outwardly
to reflect my inward prayer,
and my sincerity and respect
are an offering of devotion
to the truth of my spirit;
for I am of a supreme awareness,
and here I wander
a solitary path,
raising my arms
along with my love,
to remember the truth
of my spiritual heart,
and seeking to be embraced
within the truth,
and carried upon its wings
to soar free in this dream.
In respect may I honor life
as a gift giving in my heart,
and carrying this sacred gift
I will be nurtured by its growth,
and life it will bestow
as remembrance of the truth,
giving communion beyond my death.
I raise my arms
and give my life,
ever soaring free
in life's embrace.

Color Life Vigilant

Ever so quietly
a spectrum of color
graced my morning.
No thunder heralding its presence,
no lightening demanding my eyes,
just serenely present,
the beckoner of joy.
And how blessed I was
to glance up the ascending corridor,
for fleeting was its life,
and the moment passed by,
leaving just a shadow of longing.

How quickly
the miracle of life vanishes,
without giving warning
that we missed its call;
and life continues to flitter by,
but no one tells us
when to start collecting memories.
We lose by default,
and in compassion
the saints offer their prayers,
but pleas of love
cannot open the eyes,
or bring remembrance
to raise the mind to vigilance.

Ah how I strain my eyes,
searching the horizon
for colors gentle touch.
Once was a miracle,
could I ask for more?
I received a blessing,
but remain alert
within the patience of my heart,
to its Siren's call.

And yes, it softly graces the north,
arching a course thru ominous clouds.
The violet so vivid,
and now it grows,
it brightens,
it blooms into florescence.
But yet,
as it seemed to fill the heavens,
it fades into oblivion,
leaving my heart
both joyous and sad.

Such are rainbows,
the heralders of life,
and burgeons of death.
They are the soul of the sky,
captured in hidden embrace
within its crystal heart,
but when the light
can be refused no more,
they bloom effervescent,
unabashedly displaying their love
in songs of color.

To you, my rainbows,
I can say in truth,
that my quest is giving direction
by your arms reaching wide,
guiding my light into your radiance,
and I offer up my fealty,
and in vigilance
watch the sky,
least you call while I sleep.

Art Plate 2-27 ~ Fragrance of Life ~

Kissed by the breath of life,
I reflect my own true light.
I am eternity's stroke,
finite in limitless expression,
built of light
and cast in time,
walking the pure land of consciousness.
Each tree sings this truth,
each flower echos my heart;
and this land,
giving of purity,
is my very self in communion.
Reflecting the truth,
I am the sincerity of its word,
the respect of its life,
the humility of its power,
the integrity of its soul.
I am the breath of life eternal,
gently nurturing the creation of love,
lifting the seed of life
to bloom fragrant in compassion,
firmly rooted in Earth's wisdom.
Tenderly I embrace
that which enfolds me
and gives me life,
it is recognition
of my own soul.
All reflect the same truth,
and the fragrance
of each delicate bloom
is the heralder of remembrance,
and giver of spiritual life.
Oh how blessed
is this rare opportunity
to rejoice in breath, as
the fragrance of life.

Art Plate 2-28 ~ Freedom's Grasp ~

The miracle lies hidden within you, as the very breath of life, so grasp its expression of wonder, and embrace it to your heart. Immerse yourself fully into the challenge, and live it with gusto and strength. But here a pilgrim must be vigilant, and not cling to this dream as being the truth of their spiritual reality, or they shall lose their chance to journey in freedom. You are of spiritual essence embodied into manifested expression, and if this remembrance be used to order the priorities of your living awareness, then you are free to wander this realm of individual consciousness, and not be bound by it. Free to laugh and free to dance, in the sharing of your heart — a relationship within yourself as the dream of a living love. Embraced by truth, sincerity is the pilgrim's staff, as he respectfully communes with life as the equal but different aspect of the one reality. We all dance in a realm that is but one essence, and we can sojourn in the joy of freedom in the dream we create, if we but remember its true reality, and don't cling to its shadows of appearance. So graciously accept the gift you've given of your heart, but embrace it as an offering of temporary light, used upon a stage to view the reflection of reality, and in serenity observe as the colors weave a tapistry bound by one eternal thread, and though the strands of life bond together a relationship of form, your essence be of that invisible hand weaving its pattern throughout all eternity.

Journey of My Self

On I travel,
so far, so far,
my road stretches on forever,
yet truthfully I've never left home.
And as I wander
my hands toil deep into the earth,
I must work ever so hard,
yet never have I accomplished a thing.
And as I sojourn, during my work,
I yearn to speak of truth,
the sharing of my soul,
the giving of my heart,
yet never do I say a word.
Through speech and work, and on my path,
I have pointed to a truer realm,
and to this higher plane I look,
yet I never see beyond my Self.

Thus my course
has been an inward journey,
and the work one of sincerity;
the truth I speak is but my laughter,
and the realm I vision
is the miracle of my Self.
How wondrous to walk softly
upon a remembered dream,
and feel of its fabric of shadows.

This journey of sincerity and laughter,
in the recognition of my Self,
rings deep in truth,
for it is my heart,
born as soul of one essence;
and I must echo that Reality,
as eternity softly beckons me on.

~ Meditate on This ~

Days will come and days will go - some we understand, and others remain a mystery. Acceptance does not mean one must understand, for we are spiritual consciousness observing our shadow in wonder and awe. Our own reflection is cast upon the mystery of perception, and we are the eyes and breath of God. To much effort to understand brings fatigue; it is enough to observe and let understanding come of its own, and in the meanwhile dance to the music of life abundant...

~ ~ ~

This moment has lasted all of eternity - a paradox for the mind, but a blessed reality to our spirit...

~ ~ ~

There is a reason to rejoice, for you are alive as the miracle of God... Did you pass over this truth trivially - just think of the significance of this statement, and truly rejoice!

~ ~ ~

Spirituality can recognize but one joint consciousness. We are all equal in spiritual essence, and live thru the same breath, thus no one can be excluded from joining into remembrance of their divinity. Spirituality is all inclusive, all embracing, it is the world that in forgetfulness divides us into the duality of exclusion...

Wanderings of The Heart

Mt. Lassen National Park ~ June 1981~

One of the greatest blessings is ignorance, for thru our lack of knowledge we sometimes go beyond the limitations our mind would normally set, if it but knew the folly of our endeavor.

My first years of exploration where marked by ignorance of my abilities, and also of the conditions of limitation imposed by nature. So I often tried feats that were not only foolish but down right suicidal, just because I didn't know that nature frowns on certain physical attempts. But my heart was pure and my mind firm, and this integrity of intent allowed me to get away with my foolishness, and by the grace of my attempt learn that limitations can be overcome or superimposed, but I also learned not to press my luck.

I arrived at the base of Mt. Lassen (10,457 ft.) early that morning as the sun brilliantly lighted the imposing snow covered peak in sharp golden hues. Without hesitation I climbed the closest ridge that began my attempted ascent. The trail that normally leads one up the peak was covered in deep snow, but the way seemed obvious, so I slowly proceeded up the icy flank.

No real difficulties where met along this wind swept course, and after a few hours I found myself standing atop the crest of this magnificent volcanic peak. Oh what a glorious view it holds, and best of all, the awesome Mt. Shasta stood out in a crystal claity so close I felt I could reach out and touch her. Surrounding me lay the volcanic ridges that once formed the huge volcanic peak that Mt. Lassen was part of. Snow blanketed the peak, with a few desperate pines growing in twisted clumps along its ascending ridge; and because Mt. Lassen erupted relatively recently, there was steam rising in swirling billows from isolated spots dotting its crest, where twisted slabs of black volcanic rock jutted out of the snow.

The splendid vision was one I intended to bath in for awhile, so I found a spot amongst the gnarled volcanic rock atop its highest crest, and spread out all the items I brought in my pack. My lunch was serenely enjoyed, and I felt as if nestled at home, with the rarefied air of spiritual communion feeding my soul. For hours I sat gazing upon the forest and the many lakes below, listening for the call of what area beckoned for me to explore; but my main focus was on the awe inspiring features of Mt. Shasta, for it stands as a solitary foreboding cone, isolated from the world and untouchable.

After feeding my mind with serenity, and my heart with beauty, it was time to nurture my physical body with the exertion of returning down Mt. Lassen's icy escarpment. But here is where my ignorance played its fun game of testing my integrity. My travels up to that time had never led me into snow conditions, or did I grow up ever experiencing the snow. To me the snow was much like earth, but white and slippery, and I knew nothing of its special character, and had no respect for its awesome power. Now after a decade of exploration,

I have gained knowledge and respect for all weather conditions, and especially the tremendous fury of water.

But that day, as I stood atop Mt. Lassen, deep in ignorance and full of faith, and feeling the strength of my spiritual power, I looked at the ridge I had ascended and then looked at the sheer flank that dropped to the valley far below, and my mind considered a quicker way to return down. The ridge would be a tedious affair of climbing over ice covered rock with the sure possibility of slipping, on the other hand I had a nice snow covered flank that stretched from the very top of Mt. Lassen down 2,500 feet at a 65° angle with no obstacles, and all I needed to do was ski down its side. I had seen people ski on television, but I never had been on the snow myself, or had I ever ice skated, roller skated or water skied. The vision of snow stretched below me totally unbroken, which gave me a visual distortion of how great a distance I was really looking at. My decision to attempt to ski down the flank was finally influence by one significant sight, for I thought I could distinctly see the tracks of other skiers toward the bottom – there appeared to be nice thin groves going straight down the side, so I figured if they could do it, then I should be able to learn.

I took my leap from the top and immediately realized my error, as I desperately tried to stop my extremely rapid descent. The angle of the snow was far greater than I realized from the top. Even though I had tried to stop as quick as possible, I had already decended a hundred feet, and as I stood there

with my legs buried in snow and my
shoulders touching the side of the
severely angled slope, I realized that I
could not go back up, and I was trapped
into the position of having to go downward
whether I wanted to or not. My spirit was
still firm, and as yet I didn't know of the
dangers involved, so I figured that I
would try to do some sort of roller skating
motion down the mountain. I jumped out
of my holding position and let my legs
sort of run and slide as I attempted to
ski on my boots. But I hadn't gone but
a few hundred feet down when I had to
try to stop, because for some reason the
skiing effort was totally exhausting me,
and I was panting for air as I came to
a halt. My precarious position on the
snow covered flank now all of a sudden
struck me, as I looked up from where I
came and downward to where I was
headed. Above me was like a sheer wall
with no view of the peak, but what
concerned me was the view down, for I
had not gone as far as I thought I
should have, and then it began to dawn
on me the tremendous distance that the
valley was below me. I now looked very
closely and realized that what I thought
were ski tracks were in fact the trails
left by giant snowballs at least 10-15 ft.
in diameter that had rolled down the
side leaving huge gouges in the snow,
and these monolithic snowballs were but
specks down far below. Now I had the
correct perspective, but still I saw the
only danger as the terribly fatiguing
effort it was to attempt my shoe skiing.
So once again I jumped into space
and began my descent, and I actually

was getting a good motion of skiing, but
large piles of snow started descending with
me, and I had to notice that I was creating
mini avalanches with my motion, to the
point that I was finally riding the crest
of a sizeable amount of rapidly cascading
snow. So I changed my angle of descent
so that I would go over to my right, and
this would allow the avalanche to pass by
me. This action worked and the snow did
go rushing by, but my new angle created
more avalanche action, so I attempted to
stop my descent so as to stop the
avalanche, but it now carried me along
with it. I zigzagged to and fro till I
was finally able to free myself from my
avalanche ride, and desperately tried to
stop to catch my breath, as the rumble
of snow cascaded below me.

It seemed I had been skiing down
this mountain for hours, yet not much
time had really elapsed. It was just
that the attention and concentration
required was intense, and so was the
apprehension that was building, for I
still had only gone about half way, and
now I suddenly realized a far greater
danger than the avalanche that nearly
carried me away. Now the angle of the
snow field was gradually lessening, and
I started to hear the sound of water
running below me. It had never
occurred to me that toward the bottom
of the snow field there would be rivers
cascading under the snow, and large
crevices, and also areas of thin ice that
I could fall thru to the rivers below,
and thus be trapped and frozen far
below the surface of the snow field. My
respect for snow and water was growing

continuously, but I still had to continue my descent, and my lesson.

So off I jumped, and once again my avalanche escorted my humiliated ego down to the giant snow balls below. As I approached these monoliths of ice I heard great torrents of water flowing beneigh me, and there suddenly appeared great ice cracks and crevices to ski around. The noise from all the rushing water was deafening, and now the angle of the slope had lessened to such a degree that I had to try to ski and run across the ice field as fast as I could, or I would sink into the soft snow and lose all momentum. At any time I could step on a thin area of ice and fall down to a river below, but for the next mile fate guided my steps and I finally began to reach an area where there were trees growing. At last I felt relatively safe, but at the same time it dawned on me that I didn't know what direction my van was anymore. I had paid no attention to my course down the icy slope, for survival was the primary issue, so now I stood pondering as my body slowly froze, instead of the nice, quick icy grave I just skiied thru. But heck with this nonsence, off I set a course that I felt had to be close. It is very difficult to make your way thru thick trees while falling into deep snow drifts continuously. My knowledge increased, and so did my conviction to live in greater respect, humility and awareness. It took some searching but I did find my van, and when I looked back up the slope I had just descended, I felt awed and amazed at the attempt my physical nature just accomplished.

There wasn't a mark I could see on the mountain, yet I knew of the struggle for survival that had ensued. And because of the experience I had found within myself new strength, not a physical strength of victorious action, but a spiritual strength of respect, sincerity and humility. My intention to attempt the feat started with ignorance, but my conviction to live life as a spiritual challenge brought greater understanding of my true Self. No marks were left on the mountain, they were all left in me; as I raised my head humbly in the knowledge that my spiritual essence was undying, and that my true Self was guiding my way, and the physical was only an adventure of the moment, to be lived and recognized as an avenue of challenge. The experience brought knowledge to live in the truth of my spiritual, and I found within me new wisdom, beyond the fear and limitation of a selfhood. This was the beginning of my lessons of realizing the ways of a spiritual warrior, and this first lesson was to live in the light that 'today is a good day to die', and thus I could live beyond the limitations of my selfhood, and in this freedom I was a spiritual warrior.

Art Plate 2-29 ~ Balance An Light ~

Art Plate 2-30 ~ Essence of Power ~

A warrior lives in the power of that which gives him life. Though power uses an eternal manifestation to express its creation of energy, it is really a core of spiritual essence that embues the gift of its strength; and it is with this internal essence held deep within the soul that the warrior establishes a communion, even though it be one of limited physical relationship. I run upon the surface of life's heart, absorbed in its power, radiating its love; and every warrior is in awareness of the truth that bestows breath, and uses life as a vast shore, running in freedom as the challenge of infinite expression; always in remembrance that he is one with life, and embraced within the ocean of its totality, yet floating in the recognition of self awareness. This is the cycle of life, held in balance by the polarities of freedom and acceptance. And here I run to death's awaiting arms, only to realize that all embraces are that of Mother.

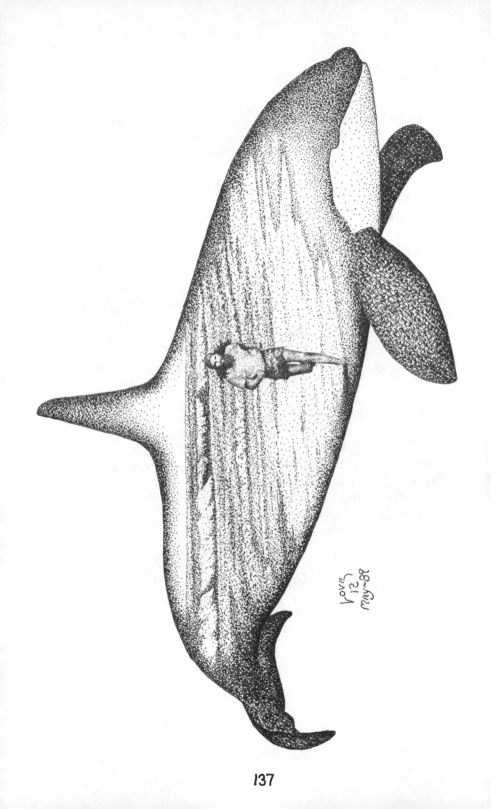

Calmly & observe the crash of activity which builds this world of desire. All must dance in this realm of tempestuous rage, for nature is an explosion of energy, and there be no refuge for the weak of heart. So on this play rages, and yet I sit calm encompassing its power, for I am not an actor captured in performance of a serious drama, I am truth spoken in freedom as life eternal. I bespeak the spiritual principle which allows the play to crash into action; and sanctuary is given thru remembrance of my true Self, which allows this truth of spiritual reality, to guide my steps to fall gently in a realm where miracle fills the heavens with wonder. All about me are the tears of uncontrolled clamor, yet truth is present, and no one is excluded from sitting within its radiant light. I am not blind or deaf to the struggle of those in forgetfulness, but can I stop my steps and halt my journey, as I sojourn within a truer realm, where the din of fear is not present. For here the birds ring in effortless joy, and freedom tastes of sunshine; and here I walk in peace, observing this parade of consciousness, letting the dream unfold, as it dreams other dreams...

Grasping Knowledge as Power

Recently many sincere people have been asking me the same question, "how does one rise above the mundane, and rest in the consciousness of their true identity?" They ask this question in a hundred different ways, for it is the ultimate question of this long and winding spiritual path – how to leave worldly attachments, concepts and fears, and live in the truth of their spiritual true nature (or how to be a spiritual warrior). There are sincere people who have studied and dedicated themselves to spiritual realization – they have done the gamut of ritual, prayer and meditation, and know the words expounded by the Masters, and yet they still have not left the desire to maintain a selfhood behind. Many have tasted a glimpse of this pinnacle of consciousness, but still cannot fully awaken to live the reality of their true self in a moment to moment expression, which becomes the unceasing prayer of life.

Here they stand, having exhausted all effort, and looking for that final question to be answered. But here at this final crossroads, which can last a short time or extend throughout the rest of their life, no one can step forward and give them the answer to a question which cannot be asked of others. No one can intercede for them at this moment of longing and hope, for it is a time when one looks for their true identity, and thus they stand alone in their quest, and reach their hand out only to phantoms. Nothing exists but a dream of their selfhood, thus they can never find an answer, or a person to question within this dream of swirling shadows, for realization is an awakening—it is the moment one awakens from their dream to realize the reality of their being. It happens when the time is ripe, and all expression after this startling moment is a simple and natural communion of the true nature they were looking for. None of us have lost anything, or do we need to gain anything, it is a matter of being that which we already are.

But here I will attempt a few words of compassion to perhaps provide a knock on the head, to help those who persistently ask others to pinch them in order to wake up. I must first back up one step and comment on one hinderance, and that is that most people do not recognize the difference between understanding and realizing. Any spiritual matter can be understood by almost anyone, if studied under the guidance of a competent teacher, but this knowledge gained thru conceptual thought is just a memory bank stored in the mind, and does not have the effect of initiating action that the selfhood has accepted as wisdom. The mind becomes cluttered with conflicting and paradoxical teachings, and in confusion expounds this questionable knowledge thru a selfhood built of concept, but the heart always knows the truth, and this knowledgeable selfhood cannot fool itself as it stumbles over its own understanding. While the ego tries to impress the ignorant with enigmatic dogma, the heart beseeches the Masters to please lift them to a higher plane; thus they continually seek enlightenment from their knowledge, and even know how it deludes them with its concept. Realization is simplicity itself, for there is no need to understand or master a selfhood that has no true reality. Realization is the living of the truth of what we are, while knowledge is the study of concepts of what we might be. A warrior has no time or interest to embrace illusions, and create a quagmire of diverse problems which demand solutions – it is the mirage of ego shouting out to Reality to pay attention to it. Realization is directly grasping the perception before us and communing within its mystery, ever aware of the miracle we are, and knowing all is 'one'. Understanding is speculating this premise, while relating it to a selfhood that worries and ponders over the concept, as it continuously clings to its desire of awakening.

This much has been said by thousands of masters, but words cannot provide the pinch a person needs to awaken. Words at best can only help make the complexity of knowledge more simple to understand, but it requires a selfhood to comprehend, thus words and knowledge can never undo a selfhood.

So please understand this point, the very selfhood of you that is trying to understand spiritual realization, is the only obstacle that is preventing this same selfhood from realizing the Self. It is a matter of allowing the illusion to slip away so that the Reality can be seen as 'One'. It is much like waking up to find that no selfhood ever existed except in a dream, and now one stands unconcerned, without desire or attachment within a reality which is the oneness of all. It is to awaken from a dream and realize that one was dreaming. There is nothing that need be done to awaken, and nothing to accomplish after one awakes. Paths and goals are the selfhood, and are the very stagnating factor preventing one from being alive in this moment.

But I have said nothing, and the question still is present—"How do I wake up?" Waking up is a very simple matter of being convinced of your own reality. Many have made it the priority of their life to understand the reality and gain knowledge of the truth, but few actually are convinced of this actuality. Fear, concepts and desire keeps the truth as a premise to speculate over, and when one is finally fully convinced of the reality of his spiritual being, he simply wakes up and lives it—it is what is called the ripe ego. No one can actually convince you, not with all the words in the world, but each of us can grasp this conviction by ourself, and see the truth of it with our own heart. Seeing the truth present in someone else's life, or hearing of the truth does not convince us, we must claim this truth for our very own, thru the power our heart perceives with. Thus the key to waking up is this—we must claim our knowledge as power. That is to say, we must accept with our mind the knowledge we have, and be convinced of its truth. Then we must claim this knowledge as the power that is our reality; and finally we must grasp this power with our heart, and live it as the prayer of our life. No one can grasp your power for you; masters can provide knowledge and give incentive to learn, but only you can grasp this knowledge as the truth, and release the power within you to live this truth as the reality of your life. It is extremely simple and requires nothing but recognizing your true self, and living in its light. You are not to understand a process involved, this is a matter of allowing your heart to accept the knowledge of your mind, and live it with the power it already has. You lack absolutely nothing, and what you add as a selfhood only hinders. The selfhood has such fear of standing alone and diving into the abyss, but the actuality of it is as a drop of water falling into the ocean of oneness — you must stand alone to become part of the whole, and leave a separate identity to rejoice in your true identity. Fear is your great deterent, and can only be overcome by conviction; your only priority must be spiritual realization, and thus your heart will subdue those longings to be a selfhood. Have no fear to be what you truly are, and claim your heritage of spiritual power. With respect, love and sincerity open yourself to truth, and allow your heart to touch the eternal place within you. Don't analyze what I've written, this is the time to drop thoughts, concepts and desires, and live serenely the truth you are. Let your actions flow in freedom, and go out and smell the flowers — see the incredible wonder, and rejoice!

~ Meditate on This ~

The greatest game the mind plays is to search for itself by observing its own workings. Spiritual paths lead one into a quagmire of investigation, and you cannot go beyond the limitations of the mind, by using this same mind to decipher your true nature – you merely build a concept to embrace, and spend your precious time in its shadow...

~   ~   ~

We all establish artificial criteria to order the importance of our life...

~   ~   ~

Remember that most teachers and masters started off confused and ignorant. Their condition provided a catalyst for change, and also a perspective from which to teach. Everyone has the same equal opportunity to reorder their priorities, and thus allow their consciousness to evolve into deeper understanding, and bring remembrance of their true nature within life's expression. Your integrity and sincerity are your key to spiritual growth...

~   ~   ~

Do not place the burden of your understanding upon another person's shoulders, they are trying to take care of themself, and sometimes not very successfully – life is our responsibility...

How should a spiritual soul express their remembrance of divinity? Should they wave a banner proclaiming the knowledge of truth? or set about the task to reform the world about them? One immersed in their God nature sees the truth of one Reality as the ultimate play of consciousness, and in this realization they commune into harmony with all of life's expression. There is no need to verbalize truths of limited knowledge, or change that which appears to have lost its balance. One re-orders their priority to express their God consciousness, and allows all expressions of life to rest in their varying stages of awareness. The eyes now set firm into a gaze beyond the relative, and view the depth of infinite vastness. The fear has left, and only a serenity found in freedom remains as their relationship with the world. And deep in harmony with the balance of the universe, their energy now fluoresces to reflect their consciousness abiding in remembrance of truth eternal. To find one who lives in spiritual realization is not a task for the eyes, it is the heart that guides one into their presence, for our Godhood is a communion shared.

147

Parable ~ Through, not around

A warrior and a young man were walking through a dense forest. As they walked the young man asked the warrior many questions, like, " my mind is so restless, could you give me a mantra to help quiet it?" To which the warrior responded, " yes I could, but you would cling to it and form an attachment to an exterior method that doesn't go to the heart of the problem." The young man then asked, "well could you suggest a yoga or other methods to help me to realize my true nature?" The warrior answered, "yes, but you would cling to this desire for realization, and the methods themself would eventually form a great barrier."

As they walked they came to an area where the bushes were very thick. The young man stopped and pondered as to their course while saying, "well, now how are we going to get around these bushes?" The warrior immediately grabbed the young man by the shoulders and spoke intently right in his face, " don't go around the bushes, go through them. This is just like the questions you've been asking. You want to know methods and means to arrive at a goal; you're looking for a course to follow where someone can dictate your actions. You are not going to the heart of the matter, you're just playing intellectual games with yourself. The real gist and heart of the spiritual quest is in simplicity – it is the dedication of being true to yourself, and ordering your priorities around an attitude of spiritual remembrance. Above all its being thoroughly convinced of the reality of your true nature, for you are a spiritual being of the one Reality, and all the methods and rituals are for those trying to convince themselves of this fact. Don't beat around the bush and look for a way around the truth, go right thru the delusions of your concepts, right to the heart of the truth, in other words go right thru the bush." And with that the warrior gave the young man a mighty shove and sent him reeling thru the bushes, while the warrior laughed in delight.

~ Meditate on This ~

We like words of wisdom only when they do not conflict with what we believe...

~   ~   ~

I know something, but I forgot what it is...

~   ~   ~

A dream is a play of the mind,
   it reflects our own thought.
If we are reflected on God's mind,
   then we are a dream, are we not?

Art Plate 2-33 ~ Center of Calm~

The world turns in tumultuous activity, for this be the realm of desire, where the energy of manifestation spins an illusion of incredible complexity — I stand amazed, for its power is awesome, and the force uncontainable. Yet here I sit in the calm of the tempest, watching the wave roll as it crashes upon its ignorance. I have no interest in controlling the powers surrounding me, I need only abide in my true spiritual self, and allow manifestation to spin its course of creation and destruction. If I allow my consciousness to spin with its flood of desire, I will surely be drowned; for fighting to control life is a most foolish endeavor, and one where death is the urging companion. I sit firm in the midst of life eternal as the essence of God I am, communing with life, and embraced in remembrance, and here I sit in the eye of the hurricane, and watch the world spin about me. What joy it is to feel the power crash around my form, and feel the mist of its vastness, as I remain centered in the curl of its wild torrent. I am the calm of the hurricane, and watch this play of life, dancing in the joy that my serenity has brought, and remembering always that I am really none of it, yet contain it all.

151

Art Plate 2-34 ~ Serenity ~

Wanderings of The Heart

Big Sur Coast ~ March 1982 ~

As winter approaches, it is time for me to slow my travels and digest the experiences my adventures provided that year. For the past eleven years I have journeyed to the coast south of Big Sur and basked in the sun at various spots along the cliffs, watching in serenity the ocean rise and fall.

One favorite cove of mine is on a bluff which rises twenty feet above the churning waves. The cliff is solid rock, and I park back ten feet from the edge, because when the big storm waves come rolling in, they blast the cliffs and send plumes of water and mist cascading down on my van. There is no sleeping during the big storms, for the winds rip me at fifty miles an hour and make my van quake and shiver like a toy boat tossed on an angry sea. It is an awesome sight to see 25 foot waves racing straight at you every 15 seconds, only to dissipate as they crash into the bluff, shaking the rock and sending a churning splash of foam and water up 75 feet into the air which plummets down on my home with considerable force. Yes, I could move to a spot that is quieter (and safer), but the storms are awesome and a wonder to behold. The power they display is to magnificent to describe in words, and must be seen to be believed. And after the storm subsides, the big waves still continue to blast the coast with furry for several more days, and what a treat to see the sun blaze its florescent light thru the crest of these giant waves, as I watch the spectacular show from the warm, golden sands.

For a few months I stay along the coast, walking the quiet beaches barefoot and in shorts while the rest of the country bares out the winter cold. I am a lover of sun, and winter is a time of rejuvenation and serenity, where I poke thru tidepools and do Tai Chi on the sandy beaches, and walk in timeless no mind as the days drift endlessly into the rising tide of a glistening sea.

Doing Tai Chi barefoot in the warm sand, with the waves timeless melody lapping at my feet, provides a rare experience of serenity. No thoughts are present as the body flows in harmony to an inner rhythm of the soul. It is not only a balancing of the physical body and a tuning of the artistry of movement, but also a balancing of our inner rhythm, and sets our consciousness into a meditative mood that orders the priorities of our life around a truer sense of heart communion. It is a space of action without volition that brings a balance to both heart and mind, and as the ocean sets a rhythm, I harmonize into its ceaseless balance of ebb and flow.

Each day I walk along the shore, and though I've walked the beach so many times, I am always aware of its unique character, for the ocean is so vibrantly alive, and each tide pool is a complete world of its own. The beach itself changes continuously, as each storm re-arranges the landscape and alters the bays significantly. But what provides my greatest joy is the variety and quantity of sea life. I recall the day that I crossed one bluff to come upon a large sand beach, and there before me was at least 2,000 sea birds of every type imaginable. A grand gathering of feathers, and my presence brought darkness to the sand as the wings of thousands of birds blocked the sun. On so many occasions the seals have followed me as I walk along the shore, and in one special cove hundreds of seals bask on the rocks as I sit amidst their gathering, and they seem delighted to watch me as I do Tai Chi. This area is still very untouched, and the rock promontories hold tidepools that are especially abundant with life. And of course the whales are just incredible to watch; they migrate during winter and pass very close to the coast where I park, and it is not unusual to see a dozen or more at one time. But of all my whale watching days, none will ever compare with an amazing incident that happened the spring of 1989.

I was slowly dragging my feet thru the warm sand, with the waves gently providing musical accompaniment, when I looked out into the bay and suddenly saw something extremely large descend into the water. My eyes popped open and I stared at the spot to see if I was hallucinating. But within a minute I once again saw the back of a very large creature arch to the surface and then descend. It was only 100 feet out into the water, so I approached the waves to get a better view. There it was again, but only 75 feet from me, and with no mistake it was a whale. Another dive and up once again, and now only 50 feet away. This is crazy I thought, what is this huge whale doing coming right into the surf where it is so shallow. But there he was again, and so close that I could have stepped out in the water and touched him. He was now right in the breakers with his belly on the sand. "Oh no", I thought, "is he going to beach himself to die?" And there he was right on the sand next to me, a humpback whale, with the last wave rolling out to leave him nearly totally exposed to the sun. But with the next wave he gave a powerful push with his tail and flippers and was once again in the shallow surf. He now moved back and forth in the surf, apparently eating something, and this continued for about 15 minutes with him no further than 10 to 25 feet from me in the gentle surf. I was just flabbergasted to say the least — I've never seen anything like it. But as the ocean rises and falls, so do all wonders, and my whale friend slowly began to go further out into the bay and there he cruised around for another hour, and finally headed out to open sea where I saw several other whales join together as they made their way north. That day stands out so unique, and I truly was blessed repeatedly, for on my way back to my van later that day I came across an area of cliffs where the waves were crashing with incredible furry. Fifty foot plumes of water were cascading down on the rock bluff as each wave smashed into the vertical wall. I watched the show for an hour, and every wave was different in its explosive furry. I had to sit as close to the edge as possible, being a child at heart, and of course a giant wave finally came bursting in and I got nailed by the plummeting foam. Now being quite wet I continued on home, but another grand show was awaiting my presence. I was walking atop the 50 foot bluff with a series of small coves below, and there in one of the coves was a sea otter floating on his back eating sea urchins. So I watched my brother, for I dearly love their precious antics. As I sat gazing at him I caught movement in the next cove, and surveying it I saw two more otters playing dunk and swim. I now looked back and forth at all the coves and to my utter amazement I saw 7 sea otters. I've never seen so many otters at one time, they are actually quite rare. What joy it is to watch their games and the skill they display in surfing the waves. I watched until the sun forcast the last show of that incredible day, for then I was treated to a beautiful sunset of reds, oranges and purples. The ocean sunsets are so wondrous, each being a unique signature of divine artistry. So many I've seen, and yet I still sit in anticipation at each glorious display of fractured light. Blessings have fallen on so many days, from mornings lavender light to the closing rays of this salty kingdom. But the nights also hold wonders, and I can recall one especially strange evening that provided both beauty and amazement.

No lights break the serenity along this stretch of coast, so each night I watch the stars, and let their glimmering presence fill my mind with worlds unimaginable. The moon is a special friend that I await each night, as it graces me with visions of longing, and on one very peculiar night the moon brought wonder to an event that has proved mysterious to this day.

My dinner was finished, so I turned out my light to serenely watch the stars. Big puffy clouds filled the sky above me, for their silver outlines were visible by the brightness of the moon behind them. The clouds stretched far out into the western horizon in puffy clumps, with black sky surrounding them as the stars made a feeble attempt to glimmer weakly. The moon was far out into the ocean concealed by a cloud and appeared as if it would set in several hours, so I watched intently expecting to see it pop out from behind its cloud any minute. For an hour I watched patiently, but the clouds seemed to be standing virtually still, and oddly

158

the moon also seemed to be standing stationary. The moon must have been full, for the clouds were lit up extremely brightly, and I couldn't understand how it was that I never could get an actual glimpse of its shining beauty. An hour slipped away as I watched the glorious array of clouds edged in silver, but then I noticed that the light began to slowly dim in intensity. This was indeed puzzling, for it didn't appear that the moon was low enough to be setting; as a matter of fact it appeared to be in exactly the same spot, behind the exact same cloud as when I first started watching over an hour ealier. But the intensity of the light continued to slowly dim till I could only see a faint outline of the cloud that was concealing its presence.

But suddenly an event happened which definitely startled me, not just wondering speculation, but sheer amazement. I had been watching to the westward horizon, and all at once I caught a glimpse of light from behind me, and as I turned I was flabbergasted to see the incredible spectacle of the moon rising over the eastern horizon. I looked dumbfounded for a minute, and sure enough the nearly full moon came up in all its glory clear as could be, and with no clouds obstructing its obvious presence. So I turned around to the western sky and there the clouds were nearly black, for there was barly a light perceiveable to illume their presence. The extremely bright light which I had watched for over an hour had now faded to almost nothing, and without a shadow of a doubt it surely wasn't the moon, but heck if I'll ever know what it was. I looked all around the sky to see if I could get a clue as to what had happened, hoping for some hint of an explanation, like flying saucers or guided missle lauchings, but I saw nothing at all out of the ordinary. The whole event was really quite simple, other than the fact that it wasn't what I thought it was, and to my knowledge enormously bright lights illuminating the entire sky aren't exactly common. But then this whole universe is one of impossible wonder, so why should I single out one miraculous event to dwell upon. This realm of elusive dreams is a miracle of expressive awareness, and all we can do as the consciousness of its reality is to observe this parade of perception with awe, respect, humility and wonder. It is not the unfolding events of fleeting beauty that binds us in ignorance, for freedom is here if remembrance be its foundation. We are walking a journey and briefly pass this land of desire, so watch in facination, but remember your true reality and never accept the relative as the truth of your spiritual essence, for we are eternally free singing a melody briefly remembered as life.

Art Plate 2-36 ~ Polarity ~

The mind looks for meaning, but there is none, so it grasps wildly toward assumption, and formulates complicated theories, to bind itself within concepts of limitation. But after all is said, and re-said, and repeated, and restated, life is still just as much a mystery as ever. Miracles cannot be explained, they can only be observed, and if one be at peace within, then joy will be the platform they watch from. Fall in love with the miracle of existence, and in fascination watch it unfold. Like a line of elephants leading a parade, don't ask where they are going, or what they're doing balanced on a pen, just join in and watch the show. All life is proceeding nowhere, born of mystery, and balanced ironically in a void. Life is not a serious drama, you'll kill your innocent spiritual joy with too many questions. Please realize that there really are no answers. Everything is relative, so who is there that can give you a perspective that is not bounded by mind and form. Why fill our tiny, little brain with lots of idle opinions — life is presented first hand to us, so bask in the miracle of its wonder, and enjoy the parade.

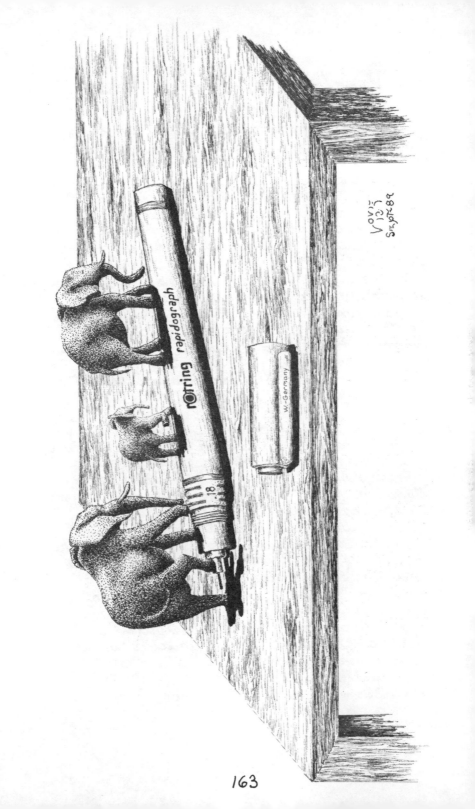

163

Parable ~ Garden of Trees

A monk and a warrior were strolling thru a beautiful garden. The trees were changing colors for winters onset, and golden leaves covered the ground. As they walked, the monk happily elucidated all the names of the trees. Pleased with his knowledge of botanical study the monk asked the warrior if he was familiar with the names of the trees in the area. The warrior replied, "yes, I know the name of every tree on this planet and throughout all the worlds of this universe, for every tree is named God. And because I know their true name, and not just the minds limited name, I have learned what my true name is also.

Comment: By naming and identifying each form into categories of separateness, we remove them and ourself from the remembrance of our true reality, and thus we forget our name also. In trying to display knowledge of name and form within the relative world, we merely demonstrate our ignorance of the reality of our true nature. There is only one substance and that is God, and we are all equal actualities of this manifested essence expressing divinity in unlimited possibilities. So use language to communicate in this relationship of sharing, but never forget who you really are, and what this miracle is that surrounds you.

Art Plate 2-38 ~ Born of Art ~

You have learned thru repeated practice,
and by coercive pressure, to take life
seriously. But I am a clown with a pin,
and its time to burst your wayward
ballon. Your seriousness is just an effort
to lend authenticity to your tears, as a
supporting actor in a drama of
forgetfulness. You take your emotional
desire to be the core of your life, and let
everything reflect its foolishness. Who
told you that you had a right to anger,
or that you have any rights at all? You
demand life to dance to your tune, and
seriousness is the glue that binds this
ignorance. Sincerity, love and respect I
speak of— they are the vital essences of
our spirit, and bestow purpose and value
within this conscious dream. Spiritual
life is sacrificed on an altar of
ignorance when an ego arises, and its
corridor of birth is expressing negative
emotions in seriousness. Understanding
the truth of reality requires a mind
unencumbered of a desiring selfhood;
it is absurd to watch the immaturity of
a demanding ego, seriously proclaiming
its right to abuse and kill within this
bountiful Earth. Observe impartial, and
watch this child of desire rampage in
its tantrum, totally forgetful of its
true spiritual nature, because it has
accepted a fantasy of concepts as its
true life, and defends them in seriousness
unto death. Watch life in fascination,
sincere in your sharing of love, but
have no desire to seek explanations
to life's mystery and wonder. Desire
merely creates a selfhood, that in

seriousness attacks the problem it craves. It takes miracle and turns it into scientific investigation, and seriously dissects it to death. A dream has no answers, it is self explanatory as itself, so let it be what it is, and no ego will arise to attack it; for there is nothing more ludicrous than a fool running mad in a mirage, thinking he's getting somewhere just because he is serious in his attempt. Seriousness is the architect of complexity, and builds monstrosities, even if there be no soul to dwell within. Spiritual life is simplicity, and no demanding ego is required, only purity of view to sincerely honor the Reality of our nature, and to walk humble in respectful wonder, as we observe the miracle unfold into itself.

So now it is time to join the parade, dancing among the clowns; and though they seriously act the role of a buffoon, the pilgrim knows the truth, and abides within the joy of his sincerity, walking serenely amidst this traveling circus, and unconcerned where the parade may lead. Life is spread before us as a grand canvas, and parade, circus and all, are the living pigment of the artist's paint. So we flow as color, dripping into life, and must accept the balance giving of the artist's hand, and leave all questions to scatter in the wind, for the time has arrived to watch in joy as the ostriches go running by, for we are born of art, and ever so blindly parade to nowhere - now here.

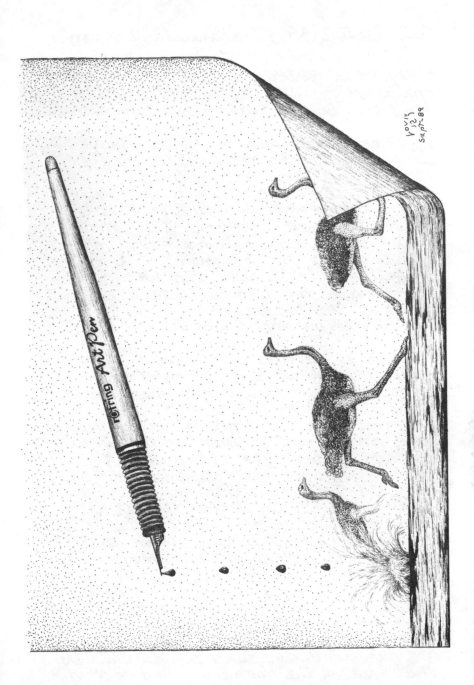

Art Plate 2-39 ~ Balance in Movement ~

Vision is distorted if you look from one direction at a multi level world. There can be no clear perspective to formulate opinions when cause and effect are woven into a fabric beyond comprehension. So very subtle is the flow of life, and circumstances dictating the obvious are hidden deep in counterbalancing energies. Thus observation beyond comment is the wisest course, and balance rests in flowing with the harmony of these unfathomable sources, instead of standing as an island to take the force of the hurricane.

Balance in movement is our life, thus relationships must flow, and concepts be flexible. Form is a continuous flow of movement – all interrelated and causing changes in the flow of the whole, yet it is no different than currents of ocean and air, presenting swirling circumstances, but not altering the integrity of the whole. Thus we continuously flow, and our only choice is either movement in harmony with the forces that flow around us, or a perpetual struggle to fight the current with a form that cannot last. Observe this universal flow from a higher view, for it has great beauty and symmetry – watch life as if standing upon one foot, thus in composure you must be balanced in vigilance, keenly aware of the surroundings, and focused into the challenge of the moment – and in this harmony there is the joy of freedom...

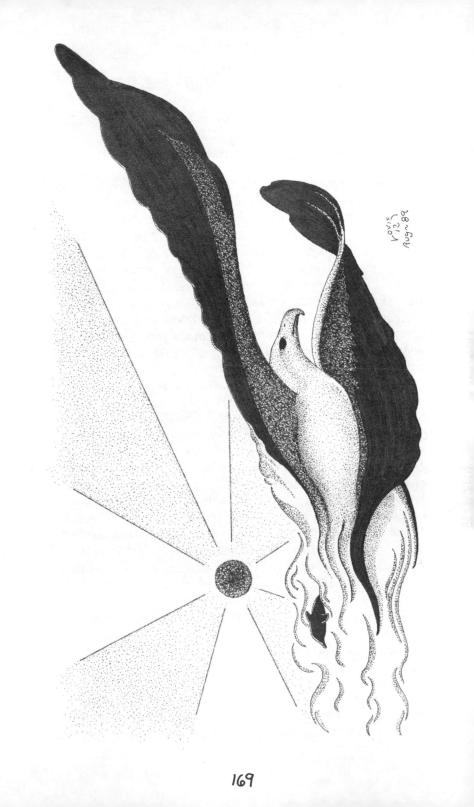

169

Wandering of The Heart

Yosemite Wilderness ~ May 1981~

Situations appear in most everyone's life where fear captures their mind, but under certain special circumstances, when the mind is transfixed in intense conviction, fear can have no possibility of entering. Thus extraordinary events have happened where a person will either appear as a hero, or possibly as an incredible fool. One such event stands out clear in my lessons as a warrior, and my total concentration built such a powerful attitude of strength that no fear could possibly enter; even though I look back on the incident and can only shake my head in amazement, and wonder how I lived.

I arrived early, but the sun already shone bright and warm, on this clear, crisp day in May. Parking my van at Hetch Hetchy reservoir, I took the trail that leads into the Grand Canyon of the Yosemite wilderness. After passing many cascading streams and several pounding waterfalls, I left the trail and bushwacked a course into an area where few people ever venture. I had no special destination, but merely wanted to find a quiet spot to read and bask naked in the sun. I followed a pretty, little stream up into the mountains, and finally came upon a flat outcropping of rock, with my little creek winding amongst the rock, and a profusion of flowers nestled within the crevices. All the open areas were covered in a rich grass lushness, and my little paradise was surrounded by large bushes for a nice touch of secluded privacy. It was the perfect spot, so I removed my cloths, and made them into a nice cushion to sit on, and layed my pack behind me. I removed my book and an orange, leaving an apple in my pack for a later snack.

The book I was reading was of great importance to me at that time, for it filled me with great zeal and enthusiasm. Its main emphasis was on sincerity of intent, and if put into practise one gained great strength of determination, and could apply it into a demonstration of personal mastery. Because I was so focused into the power it exemplified, an event ensued that I can only relate verbatim and let the reader determine my sanity at that particular instant of my life's challenge.

About an hour had passed while I devoured the words of power, and I was so engrossed into their adventure that nothing else existed for me. But from behind me I heard a noise as if far off into a distant world I left. I dismissed the activity and continued my reading without a thought interrupting my concentration. But now once again I heard a louder noise that continued to demand my attention, and the noise was not far off, but right behind me. I was sitting in a half lotus position with the book in my lap, and the stream gently flowing inches in front of me. Without setting my book aside I twisted my head around to see what this audacious intrusion was upon my sacred ground. There two feet behind my back was the menacing form of a 300 pound bear tearing into my pack.

The water container had been chewed and scattered, with my apple now in its mouth; and as I turned, our eyes met in a cold, hard glare.

My mind was completely filled with the power of determination, and thus the actions that ensued where set by my heart, with the raw nature of my animal spirit to set its course. As I turned and saw the powerful form of the bear towering over me, I immediately screamed out my warning of challenge to its intrusion. My outburst did not frighten my adversary, for it dropped the apple and grabbed my pack in its mouth, and headed off into the bushes at full speed, with me running after him shouting my challenge. A bear can run thru tangled, dense bushes much faster than a naked, gangling human, so I saw the futility of my chase after a short distance and stopped. Sure enough the bear stopped its race and dropped my pack, and began searching thru it for the food it felt must be within it. I figured I would get my pack when he was done, so I ran back to my cloths and quickly put them on. Just as I was tying my boot laces, I glanced next to me and saw the apple that the bear had dropped from its mouth. There was no other food in my pack but this apple, and since the bears teeth marks were in it, it knew that the apple was back here, and any second it would be coming back for it. As these thoughts flashed thru my mind, sure enough the bear came crashing thru the bushes at full speed straight at me. My fire was burning at full blaze, and I picked up the apple in my hand and ran as a maniac straight at the bear. We were but 30 feet apart, both racing at collision speed for an encounter of death. Split seconds passed by as eternity as we came foot by foot closer to our disastrous collision. At 10 feet apart my legs were racing and my arms flailing like a banshee as I brandished the apple he desired, and while at full speed I jumped in mid air to crash into the expected fur, claws and teeth of my adversary.

But powerful conviction has a strength of its own that sets fear in the heart of its opponent. For as I flew through the air, the bear slammed on his breaks and spun on its heels all in one step, and began to run in the opposite direction back into the bushes. My momentum carried me to within a few feet of its rear, as I continued my hysterical screaming charge, but he began to put distance between us. So before he could get to far, I raised the apple high into the air and flung it with full force, and bounced it right off the bears butt, which didn't slow him down a bit as he continued at full speed through the bushes and out of my sight. All of which time I was jumping up and down like a raving maniac, screaming at the top of my lungs in victory of our battle. Sure the bear would have torn me to pieces if we ever would have collided, but my victory wasn't of superior strength, but of superior conviction. So on I danced and sang the glories this challenge of adventure

had presented, and my spirit was so
exuberant that at the moment flying
would not have been out of the question.
The adrenalin was flowing and my
body electric, and all the previous years
of my life did not last as long as
those brief moments of courage, or
should I say insanity.

But the play had passed and all that
was left for me to do was get my

tooth punctured pack and walk back to my van. How glorious the world of freedom and challenge are, and once again I learned another lesson of the realm of the spiritual warrior. We are not ruled by our physical nature, it only sets limitation of expression. But those limits only apply within relative action, if the individual recognizes a validity to a preconceived concept of limitation. Where freedom, love and emotional aspirations are involved, then at any time we can rise completely above any limits we have self imposed, and extend those limits into new areas of consciousness. The realization of a spiritual warrior is to set no limitation upon his experience of life, and thus always accept the challenge that this moment of eternity presents. His spirit must reign supreme in his vigilance of conviction. Even the limitation of his physical nature will expand under the conditions where the heart rules supreme, for our animal nature also has unknown resources that can be activated under times of intense concentration. We are much more than the selfhood we have built thru the ignorance of our concepts of limitation. We can rise into this higher light of spiritual integrity, and with respect and humility live within the power of our true capabilities, for we are the essence of God, and we need place no limits upon our true self.

Note: other than this one incident, I have never had an aggressive encounter in all my eleven years of travels; just the opposite, for I have been blessed with a loving communion in all my experiences.

Art Plate 2·41 ~ Challenge The Wave ~

Should life be peaceful like a placid lake? well its not; life is manifested energy, and energy is active like a tempestuous ocean, with crashing waves and horrific winds. The art of life is best demonstrated by surfing the breakers and riding out their power, and using them to demonstrate mastery of your life. What value is gained in life by sitting quietly in a locked room? Life is the grand opportunity of adventure, and thru its challenge we gain experience to order the wisdom inherent within us. Verbal knowledge means little when life blasts its way thru your stable world, for true wisdom is only gained thru experience, when life tests your ability to surf its waves, and these trials come to all. Push yourself to challenge life, and gain the strength and courage necessary to stand bare in your freedom; and here in freedom's arms be calm as the eye of a hurricane, embraced in remembrance, as the wind of desire rages about you. You are free to go beyond the concepts which limit you, and bravely challenge life's blatant paradoxes. You are spiritual essence and have the ability to ride the energy of life, and use it to be master of your destiny. Accept your freedom, and let your war cry be the remembrance of your undying spirit.

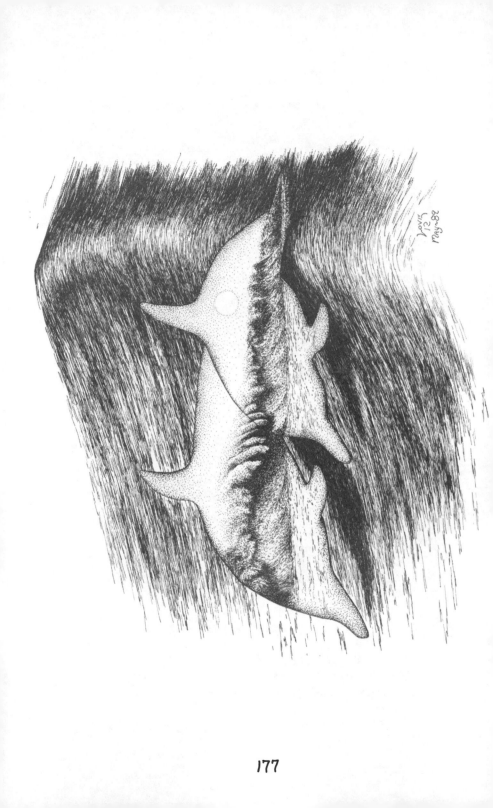

How Grand it is ~
To be Alive and Dead

What strange fire forges an ego,
from where does this pride arise
that defends concepts of right and wrong,
victory and defeat, achievement and goal?
Oh what fear binds us
to the living chains of a selfhood,
taskmaster of ten thousand duties,
and ironically the slave to its demands.
We keep our illusion alive at any cost,
even at the expense of our life.
Concept must die,
even enlightenment must fade away,
and all this frantic world of supposition
must die also,
and be lying below us as a shadow.
In our ignorance
we shall grieve for our lost pain,
but stand we must,
and walk bare with nothing but our freedom,
wielding the staff of truth
of an essence beyond, undying.
Only then can we rise from the ashes,
beyond the flame,
into its light,
and feel the miracle
that bespeaks our truth —
only then can we live beyond death,
in the truth of our divinity,
and inhale unburdened
the fragrance of our heritage.

        To live we must die,
        but now the illusion of grief.
        Stand and walk away,
        and see nothing
        but the miracle of your being.

Wanderings of The Heart

Marble Mountain Wilderness ~ Aug. 1985 ~

All hikes present challenges, but by the bent of my nature I seem to present myself with unnecessary difficulties. Where I hike there is always danger involved, but perhaps my spirit thrills in the challenge to see if I will survive one more venture into uncharted terrain.

Marble Mtn. is truly an enigma, for its name is not romanticly given, it is a factual description of its character, for it is in fact a fortress of marble. Thrusting out of the earth it caps a ridge dominated by granite. And to provide twice the mystery it stands side by side with a peak called 'black marble', and it also is testiment to fact, for I climbed them both and they stand bare with hardly any vegetation gracing their flanks – one as solid white marble, and the other a blend of black and grey all swirled with white.

Thousand foot cliffs adorn one side, as the peaks tower 4,000 feet above a sheltered valley. Though the view is spectacular from both, stretching full circle to the Trinity Alps, Mt. Shasta, the Cascades and the redwoods, the spot of greatest intrigue was as I was descending, for I crossed a rarity indeed. Upon Black Marbles lower flank I crossed an area of chasms, and there buried deep in one I found a cave of marble crystals. Oh how they glistened in wondrous enchantment, and I truly stood amazed at their lustrous energy, for they most

179

definitely carried life, and broadcast it
as the energy of living light.

August also holds the living energy
of color and fragrance, for the flowers
were wondrously in bloom, and as I
walked the crest trail, I crossed dazzling
areas of trickling creeks effervescent
with a shameless display of florescence.
And what a huge variety broadcast their
color, my favorite being one I named
Titan, for it reminded me of the moons
of Jupiter and Saturn, all swirling and
puffy. Botanical names I have no need,
but ah the colors and fragrance imbued—
my heart knows of their true essence, and
in this oneness I communed deeply with
these fields of love.

But though I found hidden lakes, as
gems cast in lush green meadows and
secluded at the feet of towering granite
peaks; and though I climbed jagged
escarpments, and traversed ridges of red
volcanic rock stretching into space, the
memory most vivid that I carry from
'The Marbles' is one where a grasshopper
spoke to me of integrity.

I stood atop the highest peak looking
down upon 'Man Eaten Lake', an azure
body of crystal set in a granite bowl.
The view lay magnificent, and how
invigorating the rarified air, like the
finest wine to a connoisseur of life, and
I reveled in the golden light surveying
a land I love. But this day was
destined to provide a challenge, and
fortitude would be needed, but also the
strength of an open heart.

I had climbed the peak by means of
the ascending valley, and I always
look for a looping course, for this realm

is so vast that it brings regret if I must repeat my footsteps - there is always so much more to see. So from the peak I decided, perhaps hastily, to walk the ridge that stretched parallel to the canyon I climbed. The ridge looked easy enough, about a five mile walk to reach a peak that rose above the valley floor where my van was parked. The ridge was unusual in that it didn't descend with the constant slope of the valley, so though I started the ridge at 7,000 feet where it joined into the granite backbone, by the time I reached 5 miles out its razor back, it was still at 7,000 feet and towered over 2,000 feet above the valley floor, and I figured I'd find some way down-perhaps an over wishful hope. But I've walked hundreds of ridges and made thousands of descents, so I just trusted to fate.

I got my first omen of the ridges strange character when I had only gone a quarter mile and came to a double faced sheer rock escarpment. On both sides of the razor ridge was a sheer cliff, and I debated turning back, but opted to mountaineer my way across the rock face - an exciting but dangerous manuver. The next few miles held tedious rock hopping and climbing; the ridge was a torture system, and its no surprise that I found no signs of any trails. Several times I came to sheer cliffs, and since the valley floor was steadily dropping, they became increasingly higher and thus more dangerous. I rarely was on dirt, but always continuously jumping from boulder to boulder, and up and over rock pinacles – it became a very tiring affair after several miles, but rock hopping is my specialty, and I was actually enjoying immensely the grand episode. But fate rose to strike quickly.

As I leaped from rock to rock, I was in midair in the middle of a jump when there in the exact place I had to land my foot was a grasshopper. I was on loose rock, and the stone was delicately balanced, and only if I landed my foot dead center would the rock maintain its position. But in this split second my spiritual ethics where put to the test; no time to deliberate the morals of taking another life, I just had to react from my heart. I have built my spiritual life on a sincere foundation, and one rule is not to sacrifice another for the advantage of my personal welfare; but here was a test of tremendous danger, and the body will often speak in its defense regardless of mental ideals. Yet even though the moment stretched to eternity I was destined to descend, and thus I was to find out how true I was to my spiritual heart.

Down I came and as I did I veered my foot to land to the edge of the rock and miss my brother grasshopper, but I knew the consequences. The rock did in fact shift and sent me reeling, but I quickly counterbalanced my fall as I tumbled in acrobatic fashion over the jagged rock, and fortunately only received minor injuries. But I still had miles of boulder hopping and a 2,000 foot cliff to descend, and now I wasn't at full strength, but this is the criterion the wilderness puts on all who enter, for each must reflect the strength of its character and be totally self sufficent. So I looked within the rocks to bid farewell to the grasshopper and continue on, but my pace was noticeably slower. Soon I came to a sharp peak that forced me to climb its shaded sheer face. A straight drop of 500 feet was my companion as I jumped amidst its loose talus, along a ledge just below its crest. And yet another invaluable lesson awaited my footsteps.

I have learned now to heal myself into an alert state when danger presents physical demands, but that day I walked injured and the dullness made my senses faulty, for once again an unbalanced rock was waiting for me unsuspecting. Its not that the rock gave any sign of its faulty balance, but I have rock hopped thousands of streams, beaches and peaks, and one must intuitively move and feel the energy of the flow of rock, and since I was injured I let my keen awareness drop, an error I have not repeated.

The rock beckoned my weight, and then as I stepped it cascaded over the edge and tried to grab me with it, but I fell on my wrist at the very brink, hitting in a way that stopped my fall. My arm now was injured and I lay inches from a 500 foot abyss, and though time was now getting short, I had enough sense to sit and meditate, and collect my energy for the real test of descending the 2,000 foot cliff.

But still I hadn't finished the ridge, so I put myself into a keen state of zen

no mind and let my spirit pave my
way. Soon I stood directly above my
van, only it was 2,000 feet below, and
I saw that it was a very steep drop,
but at least not one where rock climbing
was necessary. It was just very steep
and thickly forested with pines and
manzanita. Legs are well designed for
climbing upward, but descending is
actually much tougher when the angle is
severe, for one is continuously putting on
the brakes, and this blows out the knees.

So with my brakes firmly on I
started down the side, but found that
it was extremely slippery footing because
the ground was thickly ladened with
pine needles. I just couldn't get any
traction to stop in the dense pine needles,
so instead of taking one careful step
at a time to protect my injured body,
I was forced to take running leaps
and then throw myself on the ground
and slide on the needles for 50 feet,
just to quickly jump up and slide
once again. It was the craziest way I
have ever descended a ridge, but it
actually worked well, except for the few
trees I ran into. Though I aggravated
my injuries, the only real problem in
my descent was getting trapped a few
times in the thick manzanita. But I
got down and the last part of the cliff
was very beautiful, with deer amused
by my novel cliff sliding.

My van was a welcome sight, and
as has been the case for over 10 years,
I tended my injuries, heated water to
take a sponge bath, and prepared a
salad for dinner. The stars were as
bright as ever, and my mind serene,

and oh how much I learned of myself that day. Days to test our fiber arrive in everyones life, like a tiger in secretive crawl they spring upon us unexpected, yet they are the metal that integrity is forged from. Who can say they know of life if they never have tasted challenge, and have risen above the limitations imposed by body and mind. And only when death watches openly do we feel the need to walk humbly in respectful reflection. The time is brief and Death's touch is final, and how can one speak of truth if their integrity is never made an open book for them to read of its pages of trial. Though sincerity is the spiritual blood of life, one cannot know if they be true to themself if trial by life has not spilled a few drops of this life awareness. Tests will lurk amidst the beauty, enfolded ironicly in peace, but welcome its embrace, for they are vital to understanding, and their roots sink deep to nurture the growth of wisdom. One who is true cannot fail themself, for the challenge brings the sweetness of remembrance, and in truer light we see that the tester is but reflection of ourself. In the oneness there is only Reality, but even a dream carries value if recognition and dimension is given thru challenge, and therein lies the living breath of freedom.

Art Plate 2-42 ~ Leap of Awareness ~

How we fear the leap into the unknown, as if jumping into life was any different. We look from the perspective that where we are now, is the only place we have ever been, and that moving into higher states of conscious energy is a change for us to fear. We are the perpetual traveler, and evolution is the very fiber of our life. We cannot leave the reality of our true essence, for there is but the oneness, thus there is no real change or need for concern; our consciousness is a vehicle of energy, and movement is its nature. So you need not fear the jump into the bottomless abyss of awareness, just leap forth with joy into a living consciousness of challenge. Remember that your a spiritual being expressing forth into manifest relativity, and experience is our purpose, so embrace the adventure life has to offer, and accept its gift with respect. But do be vigilant not to cling, for life is a passing physical experience, and our true nature is one of awareness. So observe the miracle and leap again, beyond the limits presented. All of eternity you will dance in freedom, so remember of your dance, and sing in joy as the worlds of life go racing by.

187

Art Plate 2·43 ~ Flight of Freedom ~

There are those amongst us that travel a different direction — a solitary flight of consciousness. Yet embodied within us all is the social organism, and though one sojourns alone, there is no separating oneself from the living organism of life. Sit in a cave all your life, and still you will be the heritage of society, for there is no leaving this realm of conceptual consciousness, there are only varying perspectives from which to base one's relationship. All expression in life is a statement of consciousness; the one who shuns society is making an equal statement to one who embraces it. They both help mold the social mores and attitudes by the action they have taken, for society does not travel thru opinion, but rather is shoved along by the collective actions of consenting consciousness.

One who goes off into seclusion to live out their spiritual realization is avoiding a social responsibility. The spiritual community is the hope of moral transformation, and each individual needs to make themselves visible at times to show support for their commitment to spiritual evolution, world harmony and ecological balance. Take quiet time in solitude to find the truth of your Self, but remember that realization in a vacuum is dead. It must be brought into relationship with life and demonstrated if the seed of God awareness is to grow to maturity. Relationship does not mean that one

now fights for reform; our commitment
is only one, and that is to be true to
ourself, and share the love that this
Truth brings. Only an example of
integrity can work to build our barbaric
society, and each spiritual soul needs to
stand firm in their sincerity, and
demonstrate it — we each have this
obligation, for freedom is a dream
worthy of inner commitment.

189

Wanderings of The Heart

Onion Creek, Utah ~ Sept 1988 ~

Last night I woke to the crack of lightening, as thunder reverberated between the thousand foot rock walls. Then hail pelted my van with an undreamed of ferocity, as the midnight sky flashed with the brilliance of a noonday sun. The hail subsided abruptly, only to be replaced with a fierce cascade of rain, not a rain to nurture the crops of this parched land, but a torrent bent on destruction. Like a monstrous monsoon blasting the earth, I watched the show when the flashes of lightening would allow. The crashing round of the torrents of rain became all out of proportion, as it sounded as if the bucket was being cast down with the water.

But now it dawned on me that what my ears beheld, as I cracked open my back door, was the awesome and terrifying power of a FLASHFLood careening down the wash next to my van. Oh how blessed I was to be parked on a bench ten feet above the creek, for what had been a little trickling stream of 4 inches deep and 2 feet wide was now a raging torrent of incredible destructive power.

The rain ceased after 45 minutes of torrential onslaught, dropping 2½ inches in its brief life, so I dressed and grabbed my powerful latern and went out into the drenched midnight air to experience the power raging next to my van. At

sounded like a freight train, for the
torrent was sending giant boulders down
the creek, forming huge rapids as they
rolled their way down the river bed. My
petite creek was now 30 feet wide and
4 feet deep, with an incredibly powerful
swift force, forming rapids that ate at
the canyon walls causing them to
collapse into the river and be carried away.

Much of the canyon is extremely
narrow, and in those sections the torrent
was flooding between 10 to 20 feet deep,
but by grace I was parked at a wide
bend in the canyon on a bench, so the
creek could only flood in width and not
engulf my van. I walked to the edge of
the water, but this proved a bit dangerous
for waves of churning, muddy water
washed up at me, making me jump back
in haste. Just like the rising tide, the
rampaging flood continued to increase;
and now after only a minute, where I
had stood before was buried under water.
But what drew my deepest appreciation
for the spectacle I was beholding was the
incredible swiftness and power of its
main force. I've seen 30 foot storm waves
blast the coast, volcanos spewing lava,
and hurricane winds, but the force of
a raging river is something which
instills a deep sense of awe and
foreboding within me — perhaps a primal
response to its terrifying, awesome force.

I returned to my van and listened
to the sound of boulders pounding their
way down the flooded riverbed. The
cloud that dumped this monstrous volume
of water was completely gone, and now I
viewed a beautiful array of shining stars
out my skylights. How ironic was the

paradox of serene beauty and tranquil peace for my eyes to behold, while my ears heard the sounds of raging destruction, blasting its way as dynamite thru the fragile canyon. I slept in peace in the paradox this world constantly endows, and laughed at my frailty.

This morning is bright and sunny, and with great curiosity I go forth to survey my river, but the river is gone and all that remains is a trickling creek of 4 foot width, but of the color of pure red mud. How pleasant it is way down there, for the torrent sliced a gash over 4 feet deep into the river bottom. And how about the road I drove in on? well since I had to cross onion creek 20 times to arrive at my isolated spot, the dirt road is simply nonexistent at those crossings, having been replaced by huge boulders and a straight 4 foot drop to the little creek below.

Yes, that's right, I'm trapped here, and perhaps one day the road will be repaired so I can continue my travels; but for the present I have a beautiful, little spot to park, and lots of fantastic color canyons to explore, and enough food and water. I'm a king roaming a deserted kingdom, and my solitude is assured; so its time to laugh at the world's play, and dance to the tune of its awesome beat. And since I'm not going anywhere to start with, and have nothing pending in my life, I might as well enjoy the perception and miracle of not going anywhere right here. So its off into the sun I go, to enjoy this blessed opportunity to walk free in this realm of miraculous happenings.

Parable - Two Monks and a Twist

There once lived two monks in a small village - one was quite old but still strong and vigorous, while the other was young but very sincere. Each day they would take a walk out into the forest and silently observe the beauty of nature.

One day as they returned from the forest, they came upon a creek swollen from that days heavy rain. Standing along the bank was a young girl pondering how to cross the swift current. The older monk approached the girl and offered to carry her across the creek, and picked her up in his arms and waded thru the deep water, with the young monk following.

On the other side the old monk saw that the ground was quite muddy, so he decided to carry the child a little further. At each bend he would start to put the child down, but thought, 'well just a little further'. Soon they were back at the village, and the old monk brought the child right to her house, and with a little reluctance put the child down, noticing that the house was dilapidated. But the young monk urged that they should get to their duties.

As they walked the young monk asked why he had carried the child so far. The old monk replied that she was so pure and innocent that he felt he should try to keep her from being soiled by this filthy world. The young monk laughed and replied, " I fully understand your duty to carry her across the swift current, but once on the other side you should have put her down, for it is her responsibility to keep clean by her own efforts. You cannot keep her from walking within the very world she must inhabit, for she is a poor peasant girl and must live by the dictates that life will place upon her. The filth of the world will always be present in some form, but even a little peasant girl keeps a clean set of clothes ready when entering into her home."

Comment: We cannot walk for another. It is each persons responsibility to live to their highest ability within the world they inhabit, and allow each to do the same.

With age there seems to be a longing to keep the innocent children from having to walk in the mud of the world's desires and temptations. But this desire of the old places a different type of pressure upon the young which is not natural, and doomed to failure. The young must walk in the mud for themselves to experience its effects, and any form of protection only blinds them of the world as it is, which is necessary to form an understanding relationship. We are here in this realm to experience its effects, and it is we who determine relative good and bad, and though comparison may be the root of erroneous thinking, without experiencing the dualism of thought and physical expression, the child has no basis on which to see the play of events that are necessary to build a life of higher values.

This life is just the shadow of Reality— it is just the play of a dream of consciousness, and has no more substance then a reflection in a mirror. To try to protect someone from the effects of the world is just an effort to enforce an illusion— like trying to protect one from a dream. The effort is not only in vain, but proves not possible, for the dream is within the consciousness of the individual, and not alterable by anyone outside the individual's own mind. So another person can only manipulate external sources, yet it is not the externals which are the filth of the world. The filth is in the mind, which often is built by the collective concepts of society. In the pure mind of a child, what may be dirty to an older mind is not at all objectionable to theirs, because their mind has not been stained by worldly attitudes. But one cannot hold a child in ignorance of the filth that inhabits the minds of those around them, for the world must be seen as it is. Never try to supplant the worldly attitudes of desire into the child's developing consciousness, but allow the child the free will to determine if it is accepted or rejected. Even if it is accepted we must always remember that the child is only wearing the worldly body as clothing, and its true nature is pure and untouched by the desires which enter its mind. Just as changing clothes, each person will drop all the concepts and desires when leaving the body and returning to the purity of the Absolute. Our true nature is a perceiver which observes in curiousity, untouched by the events unfolding. There is no danger of absorbing this worldly filth of desire into our true self, for we are the pure essence of the Absolute; and even though we dance in this game called life, and get dirty like a child playing in the mud, it all washes off completely as we enter into our true home, and don the pure clothes of awareness of our spiritual true reality.

The eyes of the future are beckoning us to awake from our slumber. We must slow this mad pace that removes us from embracing the world with respect, for the integrity of the family union has suffered miserably. The bonding of a family is not in a house filled with materialistic conveniences, while the parents work a hectic schedule to try to keep pace with monetary demand. A home is built with love — its foundation is love, and upon this strength the parents nurture a new life; and in blossom, love must be the ground the child takes their first steps upon, if life is to bear fragrance. Basic necessities are simple to acquire, and do not require that the parents abandon the home and shuffle their child off to strangers. Do not bring forth a child if your intentions are to abandon it — it is the parents responsibility to raise the child in an enviroment that will foster the greatest physical, mental and spiritual development, so most importantly, the parents must first tune themselves to a mastery of life so that they can impart this wisdom to their child. Wisdom is vital to nurturing a new life, and love must be the foundation of its basis — you can only teach what you have embodied, so gain strength, peace and wisdom first, then let love bring forth a child. And if love be abundantly there, then sacrifice will also be present; but sacrifice does not mean you now leave the child, to go off and buy useless items to surround its loneliness. Sacrifice is the giving of your life to the child; to be

there to teach the simple love and respect of
life, and sharing spiritual communion
fostered of your heart. To provide simple
food, clothing and protection from harsh
weather is all the material aspects that are
necessary; the real necessity of a child is
love and togetherness — living in a tent and
eating wild berries is heaven to a child, if
parents full of love and sincerity be
there to share their wisdom of life with
them. Teach the permanent aspects of
life's truth, and not the foolishness of
running in circles after the craziness of
the world's greed. You are the guardian
of the world's hope, raise your level of
consciousness first, then with love raise
the child of faith.

Parable - Blessing of Vision

A very kind woman knew of a man who was nearly blind. Every few days she would go to his house and bring beautiful pictures to show him. She would describe the glorious colors in great detail, and even though he would get enthused, he really couldn't see the pictures well enough to make anything out, and when she left he felt great despair and bemoaned the misfortune of his bad eyes. The attempt to enthusiasticly describe the pictures was very fatiguing to the woman, and since no apparent results ever seemed to develop, their visits became less frequent.

Much time elapsed, and the woman was a distant memory. The man shed many bitter tears of self pity, but one day he felt within him a powerful urge. He was just sick of being nearly blind and had to do something about it, so he put on his coat and headed to the door, but he was gripped with terrible fear of the unknown outside his house. Because he couldn't see, he had never ventured out into the world, and now he paused at the door where his determination and fear waged a horrendous battle. But desperately he summed up his courage, and out into the world he went. He had no idea of what to do, but when he got to the sidewalk he asked some passing strangers. To his surprise they were so kind that he forgot his fears. He explained his problem, and one person said he knew of someone who could help, and took the man down the street to a knowledgeable optometrist.

The optometrist diagnosed the problem as curable, and with surgery the man's eyes would improve. So it was after a few years, the man regained his sight and devoted his time to helping others.

Comment: Showing pictures to the blind will not bring back their eyesight. Worldly people are nearly spiritually blind, and many well meaning persons who have opened their eyes for the first time want desperately to help everyone see the light they are now perceiving. As consciousness opens, one's heart overflows in compassion for those in blindness, and they earnestly want to help. So they approached anyone filled with the negativity of the world and set about reshaping them. While in the presence of the enthusiastic spiritual soul, the worldly person reacts favorably because they receive energy, but once they part the worldly person settles back into their previous state of mind. It is sad, but every spiritual novice must find out this truth for themself, that no matter how loving your intentions, one cannot give another person spiritual sight. It is up to the individual to make the first step; they must first acknowledge their blindness, and then they must find the courage within themself to walk out the door, which is leaving their past state of consciousness that fostered their blindness in the first place. In that child like purity of asking, even though they be filled with fear, there will be someone waiting to help and show a truer way. For each person in blindness there is a unique avenue provided for them to gain the miracle of spiritual sight. Once their

199

heart starts to open they will be filled with gratitude and love, and start searching for people to help, and repeat the same errors that every spiritual zealot seems to make. But after expending great energy and seeing the disappointing results, they slowly mature to a position of realizing that the only one that can be helped is one who is receptive to that help, and their sincerity is the only way to judge if they are. A person must recognize they are lost and then have the courage to reach out their hand, only then can someone be there to grasp it; and to the great surprise of the seeker reaching out their hand timidly in fear, there are countless people wanting to be the one to help.

Even though sincere spiritual novices are out pounding a beat for ones to save, spiritual realization will always be a personal exploration, and it is the individual that must provide the impetus and sincere intent to gain insight. It is each persons responsibility to find a communion with the light within them and live within the wisdom of their true nature, and no one else can give this determination, even if they want to. It is we who have accepted the fear, desire, attachment and concepts that caused our blindness, and it is only by our own efforts that we can see how we constructed our belief system, and how it limits us. Our efforts closed our eyes, and only our efforts will make it possible to open them again to the light that emanates from within. Through time and sincere effort we can raise ourself into a higher consciousness to correct the conditions that has caused our blindness.

Parable ~ The Crazy Man

There was a man who lived with lots of other people. Everyone there thought he was crazy, for all day long he would pry into everyone's affairs, and ask all sorts of nonsensical questions. He pestered everyone unmercifully, thus they all wished he'd leave.

One day a young man came to the house and began asking lots of ridiculous questions; so one old man decided to speak up, for he felt they were generous to let one crazy man live among them, and they certainly didn't want another. So he said, "Look here young fellow, what are all these stupid questions your asking; are you crazy like the other fellow?" The young man replied, "which person do you mean?" "Why that loony over there wearing the fancy uniform," said the old man. The young man laughed while saying, "you mean that you don't know that he is a doctor, and that you are all patients in a sanitarium?"

Comment: For millennium there have been sane souls who are as spiritual doctors amongst a society of crazy people. The world fights, kills, hates and destroys, and calls this normal, while spiritual souls pester this crazy world with the idea of brotherly love. Do not be swayed by societies norm, and conform to its immaturity. Spiritual awareness is the strength to stand firm in the ideals of inner harmony, which must be expressed outwardly as love, peace and respect. Always remember that our destiny is freedom, and your spiritual soul is not to be denied.

Art Plate 2-45 ~ Earth's Rhythm ~

We look at the world from a stationary position, not only physically but especially from the limitation of stagnant concepts. Life is singly viewed into limited perspectives of personal desire, building a fantasy world to encompass us in the folly of our actions. But this is not the world — it is alive with movement, and dynamic with challenge. It turns in strength, and likewise demands strength to walk its land in freedom. You cannot run from the world, you are the world — its bone and fiber, its very heart and soul. You can only run from desire and concepts, but this weakens your relationship of freedom. Walk in peace, embrace the Earth as it is, and let it guide your course as you observe its changing faces. But do you have eyes to see your course? or ears to hear the beat of the Earth's rhythm? Communion within your self brings perceptive faculties to listen with your heart to the powerful drone of the Earth, and even beyond to the very core of this universe. Physical eyes and ears fade, it is spiritual senses you need groom. The wonders of this realm are just unfathomable, but the mind can grasp so little of it, as it struggles with deceptive senses. How much infinitely broader be the scope of spiritual vision, for this awesome universe is born of your essence, and no limitations need hold us back from claiming our heritage.

Parable ~ Dance on Life

A spiritual master was walking with his young disciple when they came to a large river. The master said, "why do you hesitate, just walk across the water." "But master," the disciple explained, "I cannot walk on water." "Oh", replied the master seemingly quite surprised, "well then dance across the water."

Scholars expound religious thought,
to show how deep and profound,
yet tumble about
in an endless void,
as the wind crashes
against the mountain peaks.
Only laughter
can tear down
those lofty summits,
and only when dancing
can you walk on water.

Comment : The worldly mind builds concepts of attachment, thus a goal of attainment is always desired. Religious goals are a worldly affair, and step by step through careful planning, one attempts to reach the spiritual goal of their mind's desire. But this is not the ultimate state that each religion secretly acknowledges. Enlightenment, Satori and Realization are empty words in the minds of cluttered heads. But there is a state of 'being' that these useless words refer to, and this state has no name, and cannot be described. It has no logical steps, and no concepts can provide an avenue to it. If the disciple walks on the ground of his concepts he has the safety of his ignorance as a foundation. But freedom is isolated by the water of wisdom, and if you bring your selfhood and attempt to cross it while clinging to the anchor of your preconceived ideas, then surely you will be drowned in the depth of your ignorance. To reach no goal one doesn't look where one is going, or plan a course by concept, they just dance in a dream as the fleeting shadows pass them by, and this very state of selfless dancing is the freedom others so desperately try to grasp.

Only a nobody can tread the path to nowhere...

~ Meditate on This ~

This moment of existence is all one can influence, so set up no promising future goals to burden your soul...

~   ~   ~

Let the moment dictate the outcome of itself, and in observance dance as witness to yourself...

~   ~   ~

I'll wake up when I die...

Art Plate 2-46 ~ Opening To Light ~

We each build a conceptual shell of imprisonment. It is our selfhood of limitation, and here we desparately cling to our created world of fear and desire, blinding our eyes to the reality we are. Though truth perpetually shines, the ego effectively forms a dense shell of attachment to block the light of remembrance, and closes its eyes to insure a continuing depth of ignorance. Spiritual life is opening the eyes to see what limitations hold us in forgetfulness, and cracking the shell of our concepts to let wisdom and love stream in. We alone can fathom the depth of our delusion, for realization is a personal affair. Examine your attitude thoroughly to discover what concepts limit your freedom of spiritual growth. Contemplative reflection and meditation are absolutely vital to nurture wisdom's growth. Accept no other priorities, spiritual realization is the first and only consideration of a pilgrim, all other aspects pale in the light of our eternal life as spiritual actualities of God. Waste no time in frivolous worry, you are of divine breath; sit, reflect, and find within yourself the truth, and then reorder your life around the priority of living and sharing this truth. Not only is this the most joyous experience imagineable, but it is utterly simple. It requires only that sincerity be there for remembrance to bloom, and oh how wondrously fragrant is the communion it brings.

207

Art Plate 2-47 ~ Creating Consciousness ~

Consciousness creates itself, and once the living essence of awareness issues forth from the Absolute, individual recognition then builds a vehicle of consciousness, and all manifest blooms into existence as living energy. It is the unbriddled dreamer giving reality to a dream of awareness, where individual expression acknowledges itself. We are in the act of creation right now; every moment you create your consciousness, and your acts and physical body are but reflection of your spiritual creative awareness. Physical manifestation is the echo reaching thru portals of consciousness, and every experience is given value by the reflection of our true self it bestows. We are an uncontainable dream fathoming the depths of our infinite nature, and all experience is welcome as challenge. And since miracle produces itself, we can remember the truth of our spiritual nature, for Reality can watch itself in the freedom of unattached involvement. But yet scrapes and scars will come, and no one leaves this dream before waking up, and part of its unfoldment is the gamut of physical experience, felt as consciousness in the dreamer's awareness, but it is only a reflective feeling, and experience is only a vague explanation that points its shadowy finger at possibilities unfathomable we hold.

209

Parable ~ Crooked Snake

An elderly woman was coming home one day, when she suddenly came upon a huge snake on her front porch. Screaming, she ran to the back of the house and quickly went in, locking the door behind her. Her heart was pounding, and perspiration covered her trembling body. After some time she regained her composure, and once she was calm she started to analyze the situation. She now recalled that there was usually a garden hose on the front porch, and she laughed to think that her terror was only mistaking a hose for a snake. So she went to the front door and opened it, and sure enough there was a giant snake staring straight at her. The horror of seeing the snake made her collapse, and she suddenly awoke, realizing that the whole episode was only a dream. She laughed heartily to think that not only the snake wasn't real, but that she had not been real either.

Comment: Many spiritual people denounce this world as illusion. They steadfastly claim the dream appearance of manifest existence, and yet hold onto a concept of a selfhood who makes these claims. They expound theories of illusion, but dearly hold that the one making these claims has a core of being beyond the glittering images. If the perception is illusion, than so is the perceiver, for the perception and perceiver are one substance, and neither has an actuality beyond dream consciousness. All appearance of physical extension of the Absolute is illusory of character, and the energy of consciousness is its shadow, yet there is an essence that has a reality, and it defines the limits of a Self within existence. This play of mystery is the miracle of our true nature, for the Absolute is the dreamer of life, and we are the vehicle of awareness. There is one totality, thus dream and dreamer are one – the dream is relationship of conscious energy, and the dreamer is undefinable. What we feel to be manifested nature is illusory, but still has spiritual reality as dream substance of conscious awareness. It is our infinite nature in unlimited consciousness, and provides the relationship of freedom within expression. The energy expressed as life and death are plays of consciousness within the dream, and provides perspective and comparison, which allows for the creation of a selfhood. If existence was the true reality, then this would mean that God was in a process of evolving and changing. Path, goal and attainment cannot be the attributes that define the one totality called God. Thus our life is a dream expression using consciousness as its vehicle, and it is flashed upon a screen of desire, where we roam in the dream of creation, and yet we can never become it. And here we discover freedom, but only because the dream is bounded by forgetfulness, yet the Dreamer is our essence and remembrance is offered to those who die to the selfhood identified as dream; and all that is left is their laughter, as they remember the play they have eternally dreamed.

Parable ~ Fatso

Deep in a meditative trance, the woman was told she would have a direct meeting with God. Incredibly overjoyed, she saw a powerful man approaching, with long, white beard flowing in the celestial breeze. She knelt down to offer her prayer, but the man said, "please wait, I'm not God." "You're not?" said the woman, "but you look just like God." "I know," replied the man, "I'm the public appearance man. God is the fat one over there with the big nose."

Comment: So many people cling to the idea that God has a physical body, with an emotional personality. The word 'God' is representative of an undefinable concept, for it expresses an actuality beyond form that is the essence of this manifested expression. 'Reality' is one totality beyond verbal expression that has no concepts of graspability. And 'God' is of this same oneness, as dream of the dreamer, manifested into expression of conscious awareness where concept and desire hold a framework of relative relationship. Thus one can have a communion with God, as the very 'truth' that is their true nature, lived in a loving relationship with life in any way the devotee feels his heart express itself. So speak your life in love and tenderness to that conceptual reality that is your essence — a prayer of devotion to God or Mother or Father; but no matter how one nurtures their communion, it is still a conceptual relationship forged by desire, and one must recognize that beyond the limitation of relationship their is an actuality beyond name and form, a reality that has but one essence, one totality, one 'isness' — I call this undefinable truth the 'Absolute'.

~ Meditate on This ~

You are the reflection of your own sincerity ~ every act, every thought will reflect exactly the sincerity of your heart, thus we can read each other just like a book...

~ ~ ~

Life isn't a prayer to God, life is a prayer as God. One is outward manifestation looking inward, the other is inward realization manifesting as life. One is forgetfulness in search, the other a living remembrance. One is duality of path and goal, where concepts rules their expression, the other a simple communion. Religious practice is talking to God, but a warrior simply sings and dances as the divinity of God...

~ ~ ~

You can only teach what you yourself have embodied...

~ ~ ~

There is no spiritual practice — spirituality is a quality of life that is lived as each moment bestows awareness. You must be the truth, you cannot think about truth — you must be God, you cannot look for God...

Art Plate 2-48 ~ Sharing Truth ~

We all have knowledge to share, but always be vigilant not to blindly follow the concepts of others. Observe those around you as they react to life, and thus gain experience thru their example, not in a judging capacity, but rather as witness to order the relationship in which you wish to express your spiritual identity with the world. Life is too precious to give your heritage of freedom away to a teacher or master. A true teacher is one who will do everything possible to ensure that you remain true to yourself, in your personal expression of freedom. Their only teaching is the truth in which they live their life, and show it by example of their sincerity. A warrior will never allow you to jeopardize your integrity by calling them master, but you can stand by their side as a friend, and share the precious gift of life together. Though a warrior walks alone, he is always ready to share of his sincerity and respect, and in humility pass this genuine love of life onto those who sincerely ask. Relationship is the miracle of life, and everyone has something to share; and one is blessed if thru communion they can share the truth of our reality, and demonstrate it by the integrity of their devoted prayer of life, and thus inspire others to contemplative reflection, which fosters remembrance of their true nature of God.

Enlightenment

Enlightenment is a concept. Take any example you like of someone who is enlightened, and you will still find ignorance. We categorize every degree of consciousness, but this is the same ignorance that initially builds this world of illusory folly. We live in concepts, and thus build edifices to this ignorance by naming and classifying every degree of ignorance we have, and this especially applies to spiritual aspirants. We continually want to know where we are on the road, and where everyone else is in relation to us.

This conceptual thought is a great barrier to being content in the actuality of our true nature. All speculation pulls one away from there center, and supplies an illusory realm for them to dwell in. A spiritual concept of life is no different then a worldly concept, other than the degree of self deception which is accepted. Thus the enlightened soul who lives the highest spiritual concepts, is merely the least ignorant one around; but as long as life is lived as an effect initiated from the concept of cause, than ignorance will be the platform one stands upon to expound their words of wisdom.

Only that soul who lives pure in his heart, without thought concepts to initiate his actions, secure in his integrity without the need to verify his life to himself and others, whose only motive of existence is to experience what is before him, with no concern to past or future, living the simplicity of the moment, seeking nothing, clinging to nothing, living the freedom of being no one, only this soul could be called living there true nature; but no one wants this state of consciousness, not even enlightened souls, for it is seen as a living death.

But here the paradox rests hidden, for when one dies to life, then death becomes life. To one who doesn't look to goals or meaning, the rocks are alive. He doesn't think of himself as alive as does a worldly man — he simply 'is', and experience parades before that living essence, thus all energy is life, and he echos their expression of life as a mirror reflecting an image outside itself. He observes, he listens, he talks, but no activity carries any greater value than another; all life is equal, and all activities within it are equal, thus he sings and dances as he does whatever task is set before him — no attachment to outcome, he accepts blame and praise as equal, and doesn't allow their burden to prevent his expression of this moments folly, for everything he does is folly, and all of it is equal. The enormous difference is that he knows of and understands the folly of his life's endeavor, and all others don't. But is he enlightened? he accepts no concepts, and that includes enlightenment. He may live his true nature, but that includes the ignorance of manifesting a body of desire to shadow the reality of his true essence of being. So he lives his ignorance, and doesn't let that deter him from communing in freedom within the possibilities he has actualized.

217

Parable - Three Aspects

Once again the disciple found himself in the presence of his teacher and said, "last time we were together you said that we were the surface of the ocean, but its depths were our reality. I now understand this matter of our ego well." The teacher chuckled and replied, "I'm afraid you have misunderstood me once again, for our ego is not the surface of the vastness. Indeed the enormity of the vast depth is the uncontainable Absolute, but its surface is our true spiritual nature. Both have a reality and are alike in nature for they are equal in essence - one is vast, deep and hidden, for it has no relative nature, but the surface is our true Self of relative manifest being. It is a reality, but is dependent upon the depth supporting it. We arise from the depth to take form, much like the energy of a wave, but our essence is equal to the Absolute, it only differs in perspective.

But now as to our ego, that is yet another aspect. Come close to the water and you will see that reflected upon its surface is an image of the surrounding terrain. You can see trees, clouds and even your own face, but none of these objects are in the water or on its surface, they are but reflections of the reality. Your ego is as this reflection, it has no reality but paints pictures of differentiation upon the one substance of our true nature, like paint upon a canvas. We all have the one same true nature as essence manifested of the

Absolute, but the ego is a reflection of the mind and body, manifested of our energy. As your mind names objects and accepts limitation, these concepts build a swirling reflection superimposed upon your true Self. It does not change your true nature of Reality, it only gives it name and form to grasp to, and thus we build up, tear down, and support a continuous process of evolving an ego. It is a strange game that has no reality, yet as I said before, you can even see yourself reflected in the water, and thus the ego views itself and builds a framework of identification, and supports it with its concepts and calls this construction reality. Yet the ego's very nature changes continuously, and this indicates its illusory nature.

So the depth of the Ocean is as the ultimate Reality — it is the Absolute, while the surface of manifest form with its waves of energy is the essence which has become the individual aspect which is your true nature. And the illusory image reflected on the surface, which swirls in continuous change, is your created selfhood. If you wish to abide beyond illusion, then drop your limiting concepts and serenely watch this play of consciousness, for life is the sharing of a joyous heart, and your true essence is the miracle that allows it to beat."

Life is incredibly simple, and it takes great effort to complicate it. Man has forged a world of concepts, born of desire and attachment, and proliferated by blinded ignorance. This is the ego of man, floundering in complexity beyond his mind's limited capacity, and completely bewildered by the mystery of his life. But spiritual communion cannot be denied, it can only be sublimated and masked by useless appeals of the ego. Let the truth be fully understood that spiritual realization is not complicated or difficult, it is quite simple, for we are the very essence of the truth called God, yet man does everything possible to refuse and hide it. But what is to deny, their is one totality of existence, and you are its living breath – an awareness born into dream, observing reflections of consciousness interwoven into relationship. To maintain a selfhood in a relative world, where desire has built a carnival of reflected illusion, is what's truly difficult. But just to live pure in the heart, with a mind uncluttered by superficial desire is the most natural expression possible, for it is our true self. Don't make spiritual realization just one more complicated affair to figure out, it takes no effort to live true to yourself. Just relax into your heart, and accept your freedom — watch the sunset, as life weaves its flow of blending colors, and let your spirit rejoice in observing your remembrance of Self communion.

Wanderings of The Heart

Indian Creek, Canyonlands ~ Sept. 1988~

Life is the evolution of innocence
lost, and wide eyed as a child I was
taught this lesson of life in all its
wisdom by a little, spotted lizard.

Hopping my way across the boulders
I followed a little creek as it wound
its way along the canyon bottom. Ever
so frequently I stopped to smell the
desert flowers, once again fragrant with
bloom, and gaze upward at the rock
escarpments that towered high above
me. Willows lined the canyon floor, and
butterflies provided a most welcome
escort thru this red maze of twisting
rock, as red spotted frogs leaped from
my path. How the desert blooms
abundant when the sacred touch of
water bestows its life giving essence,
and all crowd to its edge to quench
that desperate need.

The sun slowly brought warmth to
the canyon floor, so I picked a secluded
spot under a cottonwood tree that
provided filtered shade, and a song in
the rustle of its leaves. Now joining
me on an adjacent rock was a cute,
little, baby lizard. How precious was
this petite creature, and I found it
hard to imagine how this fragile little
soul could survive this harsh terrain—
and true to this thought, proof came
slinking its dreaded appearance.

All of a sudden, a big, nasty, black
spider crawled over the edge of the rock
I was on. I had been so careful not

to scare my pretty, little baby lizard, and now this awful, gangly spider was sneaking its way toward my welcomed little friend. I didn't want to move for fear of scaring the cute, baby lizard, but now the horrible, horrendous spider was only a foot away and stealthing ever closer, so I felt I must shoo it away to protect my lovely lizard. But oh no, too late, the baby lizard caught sight of the huge, monstrous, hairy creature. The spider stopped its slinking approach atop my rock, and the little lizard, which lay upon the adjoining rock, cranked its head to peer at it.

Oh my God, what happened !? As quick as a flash the tiny lizard leaped over to my rock and grabbed the poor, defenseless spider and gobbled him up. The fuzzy, cute spider was so big that the mean, ole lizard needed several minutes to get him down his voracious throat, but after licking his vicious chops, all that remained was the poor, old spiders legs laying under the villainous lizard's full belly.

I sat there in utter amazement—this was the poor, defenseless creature I was going to protect? I learned a powerful lesson that day—our emotions are generated by the ignorance of concepts in the mind. To exercise wisdom one must see and experience life unbiased from the prejudice we have used to build our ego of consciousness. Wisdom is in observing life as it unfolds, and letting it be what it is. How simple it is to watch this world, but how difficult it is not to compare and judge it. But this is the task of freedom, where one witnesses with the heart as an active participant of life's unfoldment, yet stands unattached within action, and allows their wisdom to guide a course beyond personal desire. We must be in relationship with life, but to express mastery within it is the subtle art of walking this realm as a child in total acceptance, and at the same time to keep wisdom foremost as the remembrance of our ultimate nature of spiritual actuality. Thus we live in the balance of wonder and miracle, and in harmony, unattachedly accept the involvement of life's powerful embrace.

Parable - Free Choice

Deep within the torturous halls of hell, the devil cracked his vicious whip, as the grand taskmaster of the damned souls. Up to their knees in burning coals, the desperate souls trudged in pain, but strangely one fellow was smiling and whistling a merry tune. The devil looked intently at this care free soul and thought, " I'm just not getting through to this guy."

Comment: Interpretation of perception is one of conscious choice. Where our awareness is focused is the avenue we perceive, but it is our beliefs about this perception that determine how we understand our awareness, thus our beliefs build our consciousness. Each moment we experience perception, and it is our freedom to either accept the relative as factual, and thus build a conceptual world of desire, or we can look deeper in remembrance of the reality beyond this relative plane. We each have built our world to the exact specifications of our desire, and here we dwell in our constructed belief system. We are under no pressure — here and now is the opportunity we have presented to ourself, and we are capable of moulding our awareness to the dictates of our freedom. This play is not serious, it is only a moment of consciousness in exploration and acknowledgment of itself. You can order your interpretation to see the reality if you so chose; it is an attitude that you are free to be - this is the miracle we have given to ourself. We are free and we can live this freedom, and there is no burden to prevent us from so doing.

Art Plate 2-51 ~ Serene Observation

A warrior is a master of unattached involvement. Although he applies his heart fully into all his activities, he doesn't give away soul, for this is the sacred communion he has established in remembrance of his true nature. With love and dedication he embraces sincere effort, but does not cling to apparent results, or to the action of the attempted achievement. Freedom in expression is the real art, and any demonstration or physical result is merely the obvious outcome of personal power and mastery. Perpetual vigilance is the sustaining activity a warrior undertakes, it is continuous remembrance thru observation, within the serenity of a quiet mind, and the vibrancy of a loving heart. Freedom comes in this balance, and harmony is the only way to touch the truth of your true nature, and live by it.

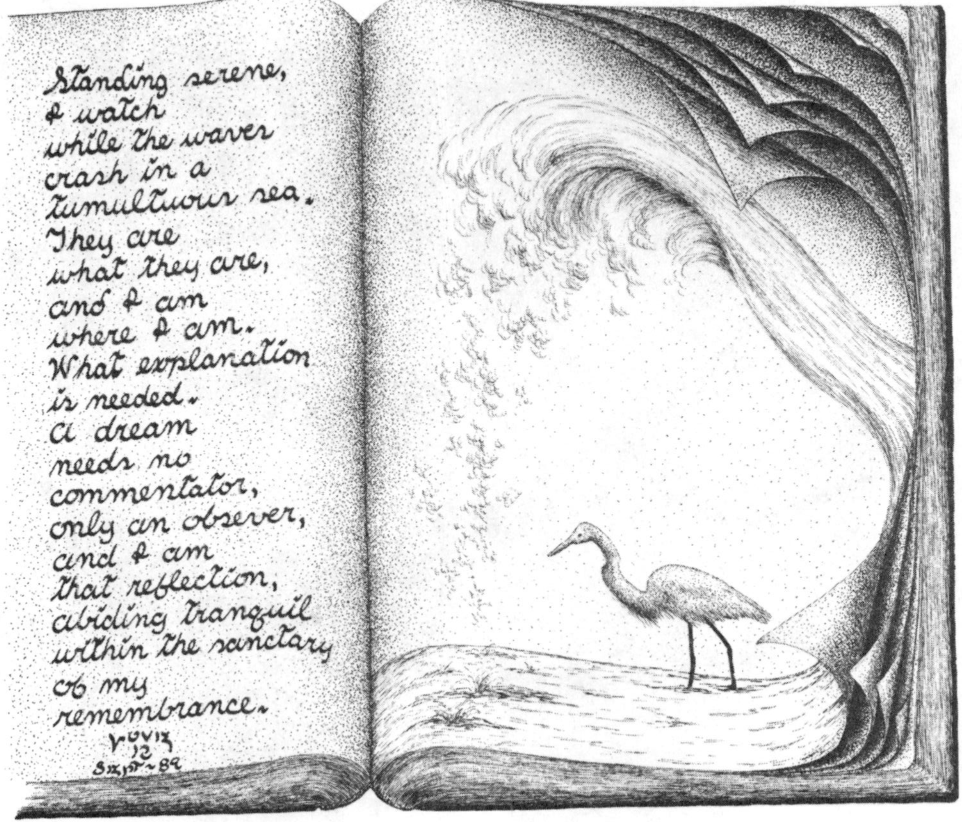

Standing serene,
& watch
while the waves
crash in a
tumultuous sea.
They are
what they are,
and I am
where I am.
What explanation
is needed.
A dream
needs no
commentator,
only an observer,
and I am
that reflection,
abiding tranquil
within the sanctuary
of my
remembrance.

Art Plate 2-52 ~ Shadows ~

Wanderings of The Heart

Trinity Alps Wilderness ~ July 1985 ~

Though the Trinity Alps have beauty
to compare with the greatest ranges of
western america, they are an enigma
with diverse character, and moods that
present changing faces of drastic nature.
For two months I hiked every direction
of its vast terrain, and watched how
the seasons gave blessings, and how the
mountains shook with rage. Dealing
out harshness, they easily jeopardize my
life repeatedly, but oh the beauty shared
and the communion they bestowed; I
can only look back at its paradox, and
rejoice in the experience given to walk
amidst its mysterious terrain.

Unexpected snow caught me bewildered,
blazing heat soaked my brow, rugged
climbs brought fatigue, and there amidst
diverse polarities, the primal, virgin
land brought me love. Thus I walked
each day along its creeks and up its
ridges, seeing tremendous displays of
wildlife and flowers — so much deer and
bear, and such lush meadows, and
panorama views so spectacular. My
adventure up Bear ridge proved its
epitome — 12 miles of hard, rock climbing
along a sheer, knife ridge dropping
thousands to feet to a pristine, grassy
valley dotted with lakes. Even 14 hours
of light wasn't enough time for this
mountaineering challenge, and the 4,000
foot climb extracted a price in blood
and fatigue. I even took the next day
off to soothe my tired body, a rarity

for me not repeated.

But a new day arrived and I hadn't climbed Trinity's highest peak yet, so off I drove to the area which would start me off toward its direction. Thirty miles thru the winding hills to an isolated trailhead, but when I arrived I received the surprise of no trail thru the tangled, incredibly dense manzanita. Earlier I had to hike on hand and knees for ½ mile thru this gnarly mass on Devils ridge, and I wasn't in the mood for another episode like that; so I drove a little further till I crossed a little creek, and it was so lovely that I parked on the bridge with the creek running under my van, and had a soothing view of the creek dropping in a series of cascading waterfalls, as it wound its way thru the pines and madrones.

Rarely do people come back into this remote area, so I was surprised when I went over to my little stream and saw that someone had altered the creek to form a lovely pool above its waterfall. Well, I had intended a hike, and I don't like being idle, so I said to myself, "why don't I just continue where this guy left off." And thus began the wondrous epic of my 'Japanese Garden'.

I got out my shovel and gloves, and surveyed the area for materials, and found no lack of perfect rocks to build with. The area sloped in a series of cascades, but had one beautiful, flat area about 40 feet long that dropped suddenly into a 15 foot waterfall. On this flat area, surrounded by overhanging trees I built a paradise. I rechanneled the stream by building rock levees, and

built a series of ponds with waterfalls—
all lined with rocks. I dug a large
pond and built an island where I
could sit, and to adorn its tranquility
I fashioned a low throne of rock, and
set before it a stone temple with altar
inside, where I burned candles and
incense. A stone walkway wound itself
around the ponds, and even thru one by
a series of stepping stones. I even
planted edible greens along its bank,
and transplanted flowering plants
from the forest to give it a garden
atmosphere. My new stream wound a
lively course, gurgling as it dropped in
a series of little cascades to give the
sound of beauty as it rounded my
temple, and here I sat each day for
meditation and food. For 4 days I
worked hard, and no gardener could
claim greater results, for it was truly
a work of art and love, and worthy of
its title, 'my Japanese garden'.

On the fourth day at dusk I was in
my van preparing my salad, and ever
so often I would glance out to view the
beauty of my finished garden. But to
my great amazement, as I peaked
around my door, there were 4 cows
quietly drinking out of my closest pond.
I looked with indignant intent, and
simply stared at them with selfish
ferocity. They looked up at me bewildered
and saw my obvious displeasure, and
quickly they departed from the garden
and continued down the dirt road till
out of sight. I stood there as the fool
I am, and opened my heart in prayer
for forgiveness. Attachment is deadly
to a spiritual expression of love, and

231

I saw the foolishness brought of ignorance when one forgets of his true nature. Spiritual realization is remembrance and acceptance, and a constant vigil is the warrior's task.

Quickly I donned by clothes and ran down the road at least a mile, till I caught up with the 4 cows, and there I humbly apologized to them for my ignorance, and asked them to return and help themselves to the sacred water of the garden's pools. They listened politely, and then I left, purged of my forgetfulness and once again breathing of pure light. A half hour passed and yes the 4 cows did return, and ever so respectfully they walked single file to the largest pool, and not disturbing a single stone, they drank their fill and then departed, as I waved a welcoming assurance of love.

The next morning I bid the garden farewell, and once again hit the road, but on my way I found the 4 cows, and stopped to bid them good day, and told them that they were the new proprietors and guardians of the garden. They understood, and I sent them my peace, as I continued my way to nowhere; and I could only laugh to think, that whoever might chance to come this way, would be in for a real surprise when they glanced over to the creek and saw a monument of love.

It is within our efforts that lessons lie hidden. Consciousness is built within the sincerity of effort, and it is its own reward, thus work is the joy of effort, and one is truly blessed to demonstrate their integrity in a labor of love. But here ignorance lies waiting, for desire within effort brings attachment, and blinds one into forgetfulness, as their selfhood clings to expected results, as the reward of their effort. Spiritual freedom is a warrior's breath, and it is deadly indeed to construct attachment to their path of love. Unattached involvement is the best way, for we must experience the unfoldment of consciousness in relationship with life, but it is a shadow of reality, and perpetual remembrance is the sword that cuts the bonds of ignorance, and sees beyond the shadow of forgetfulness. Even a warrior's love is a path that binds, thus true realization stands serene in joyous observation, watching unattached as life breathes into existence, and recognizing the miracle of its birth, while rejoicing in the mystery it presents. Freedom is the call, and we ourself are the very speaker of its words, and in the totality of this elusive reality, all the words are but one.

Photo taken by Francesca, a fellow warrior, in her wondrous garden ~ May 1989 ~

Parable ~ Mother's Reflection

A young man came to a warrior and asked to be taught the reality of life beyond name and form. The warrior agreed and brought him to a beautiful picture of the divine Mother set in a lovely glass enclosed frame. He told the young man to sit in front of the picture and look at it till he could see the Reality that was held within the picture. The young man thought this method was very strange, since he was interested in abiding in the reality beyond form, and now he was set a task to worship an idolized form, but he consented and dedicated himself earnestly.

Month after month rolled by, and all that developed was that the young man felt a pure love for the concept of Mother's grace, but he recognized no realization of a oneness with the Mother, or did he reach an understanding of his true nature beyond form.

One day the sun was brightly lighting up his room, and this caused a glare on the glass of his picture of Holy Mother. As usual he began to close the blinds so the glare would disappear, but this time he looked at the glass covering the picture of Holy Mother first, and was amazed to see that his own image was being reflected in the glass, just like in a mirror. He easily distinguished himself in the glass, and at the same time he could easily see the picture of Holy Mother thru the glass. He sat dumbfounded, for it all became so clear to him. He and the Mother were one and the same reality, and there was no separation. He had been looking at Holy Mother as separate and apart, and now he saw that he was indeed Mother as just reflection thru Her reality. He laughed at the simplicity of remembering the true nature of his being, and then his selfhood melted into the oneness of the totality of all existence, beyond name and the limitation of form. He realized all was the essence of one ultimate reality, and his aspect of individual consciousness was but the fragrance of the radiant flower, just the shadow of the dancer, just the light of the sun, and the reflection of the one Reality, for he was the dreamer remembering the dream.

~ Meditate on This ~

Just to be free, without expectation or demands is all one could ever hope for...

~   ~   ~

Oh how glorious it is to be the existence of God. No where to go, nothing to do — and here I sit, breathing the miracle...

The wave breaks,
crashing upon the serenity
of a foreshadowed evolution.
Nature accepts no dictates,
and plans are the refuse
it builds disaster with.
The eons pass
as rhythmic waves,
and stability
is a continuum of change.
The tide rises and falls,
and in its shifting sand,
we feebly build
to the echo of decaying dreams,
yet beauty lies
in the waking laughter
of time passing into eternity.
The call of each atom
longs to selfhood,
and birth gives way to consciousness;
thus the play becomes
aware of itself,
yet blinds its way in thought.
Vision needs an unbending view,
yet the dance
is a spiral cascade,
of glittering reflections blinding the mind,
and laughter deceiving the heart,
yet we spin this web of future desire,
and entangled are we by choice.
Trapped within curiosity,
watching the waves
alter the truth,
we float upon an ocean unfathomable,
observing our reflection,
shining brightly across the sea
of infinity's perpetual moment.

The tempest rages,
ferocity unbounded,
as Nature unleashes desire.
All must now reflect its power,
for sanctuary cannot be found.
Commune with the strength,
your very fiber
is built from its call,
thus you will echo thru time
as the stability forged of motion.
Yet, ah to sit serene,
the eye of the fury,
witness to tales untold.
Observing the onslaught,
our body is this wave of destruction,
yet soul beyond it,
silently viewing the devastating roll.
Tranquil as a holocaust,
there is beauty in power released;
shrinking from the torrent,
yet drawn by its silent call,
to the awesome cry
of Nature's wail.
Our form will rip
asunder the current,
and in curiousity
spirit watches on.
Another display of breath
moving in and out
thru the portal of life,
an ebb and flow
to eternity's whisper;
and are not we
the one softly chanting,
as nature dances
to our drone.

239

Art Plate 2·55 ~ Earth, of Attachment ~

We grasp a form
and trap an illusion,
and in turn are trapped
by the folly of our reach.
Opening the eyes
closes the vision,
and a beggar leads the way,
though he be blind unto his heart,
and ever deceived of the mind.
Beauty captures this dream,
and we roam amidst
a field of laughter,
held in subtle embrace
by overpowering strength.
Thus we cling,
rarely recognizing
that we have bound ourself
within a web of freedom.
There can be no stability
in clay and shifting sand,
yet forgetfulness cloaks our eyes,
in a dance
with a partner estranged.
The dream has no duality,
nor can awareness be at fault,
but acceptance
carries a heavy burden,
that none possess the strength to tear.
Yet do embrace this journey
that's forged of shadow,
but remember that energy
laughs in time,
and space fills no void ;
you are an essence beyond,
and vision is the wings of a dream,
and you are that dreamer,
dreaming other dreams.

Art Plate 2-56 ~ Fire, of Passion ~

Forged in the fire
we burn uncontrollable,
but are we consumed?
Energy strikes
in explosive blindness,
yet balance rests
in the harmony of unseen forces.
Thus the wheel turns in passion,
but desire is only its play,
always more lies unseen,
awaiting a witness.
Never does the lightening strike,
without a fire burning beneath
to call it down to destiny;
but does blind chance
rule the fate of downcast eyes,
for the light is power,
and blinds all who come forth,
least they be of valor.
Power is approached with power,
and the door be the same for all.
Mood is the holder of truth,
and accepts the power
of the lofty summit,
as the lightening flashes,
and the rocks melt asunder.
We are the very power
used to challenge our integrity,
and stoic be our countenance,
yet fierce joy
burns in our heart,
and the fire flames
forever.

243

No explanation can bespeak
the mystery of life's wonder.
It sings of paradox unleashed,
for life walks in the shadow of death,
and both steal away to mystery.
Light blooms forth
and tenderly nurtures with fragrance,
but as the blossom springs,
so does its avenger,
for death prowls in anguish,
stalking the polarities of night and day,
and ever reaching out beyond.
But irony is held in its grasp,
for life needs death to spring to seed,
and decaying leaves
are the fertile mold,
that nurture the heaven's light.
All is balanced in the hand
of mysteries wielding sword,
cutting the bonds of life and death,
evolution's spiral course.
But within the eye shines crystal pure,
depth reaching true,
mystery bespeaking miracle,
an essence aware beyond life;
but mystery is our cloak,
and wander we shall,
watching the light
turn into night,
and wondering at the stars.

245

Wanderings of The Heart

Travertine Hot Springs ~ Oct. 1985 ~

Nearly everyday I hike into areas of wilderness and explore its rugged soul. How vast is the panorama of the sun's terrain, but this realm is composed of balancing polarities, and the night also commands my presence. So as I wearily return from the days exhausting challenge, I am refreshed by a sponge bath and salad, and then once again I don my clothes to hike into the silent shadows of the night's embrace.

My night hiking has a different mood then the struggle presented by the sun's light of adventure. Though I do occasionally take a hard hike by the moon, normally my night hiking is of contemplative communion, and I usually wear my meditation cloths to enforce a slow, serene walk, embraced by the stillness of a shadowed eternity. Ten years has now found me walking within the days cocoon of darkness, for though the sun be absent from these hours, the Earth is still vibrantly alive, and shows its life force to those with ears to behold its power, and eyes that can penetrate into its soul. The stars ever fill me with wonder, no different than a meditative trance; they give no overt meaning or message, yet bestow value and purpose. The night is a paradox, and gently gives yet withholds its face.

Unlike the sun, the moon awaits in ever changing cloth, for it is as a chameleon that varies its reflection to suite its fickled nature, as it romances with the sun. She is my dearest sister, and speaks to me of power without desire or attachment; and of how to respectfully use but not to grab and hold, thus her lesson is the art of possessing without clinging, and of desireless attainment. She gives silently of her precious gifts in cool clarity, and doesn't extract a price of energy as does my brother sun.

How many nights I've walked softly upon the desert floor casting black shadows by the sublime light of my sister; letting her guide a course of inner reflection, and yet awestruck by her beauty. But she also teaches impermanence, and oh how she fades. For so soon the stars replace her brilliance, and the wonder of the heavens fill me with longing to reach out to the immensity of their vastness. How I long to walk upon each world lighted by those myriad suns, flashing a message of eternity in golds, reds and blues; I can do no more than gaze astonished at their wondrous presence. Thus my walks thru the blackness of day are a meditation of movement, and senses are only there to allow my heart to sing with the crickets call, and laugh as each creek babbles it gossipy course.

But a warrior walks in strength, and the night most definitely has power, so on occasion there arises the urge to challenge its deceptive nature, and off I go to test my integrity. Ah in fondness I can recall the night I scaled the cliffs of Bryce by the moon's brilliant touch; and the charms of Arches National Park I leaped cast in a silvery silhouette, and even up its fortress of fins I climbed; and thru the desert upon its white sandy dunes I rose to the heights of Eureka Dunes; and oh how the night wailed as I traversed Banshee Canyon, and yet sang so sweet as I decended the cliffs into the San Juan river gorge. But these tales bespeak my challenge, and here I wish to share my adoration for our balancing nature of darkness, for we are not only of the light, but also bespeak of the dark where we hold a key unseen. So I will share one gentle memory when the night embraced my soul and fed me with the secrets of contentment.

Midnight approached, and the moon lay full at its zenith. But this night was very rare, for not only was it warm to my skin, when just the previous evening frost laced the leaves in white, but instead of dressing to embark into the moonlit darkness, I stripped away to naked flesh and walked nude within the shadows edged of silver. Only a short distance this night I walked, for awaiting me was the fluid heat of travertine hot spring, set natural in twisted formations of travertine at the base of the Sierra's, and so peacefully serene was its countenance, with not a ripple disturbing its surface. Gently I slipped into its warm embrace and lay motionless floating in liquid love. Utter stillness filled the air, with occasionally a whisper of wind to gently speak of secrets held, but also vocal in the depth of silence was the full moon

248

casting brilliance upon the twisted rock of ghostly travertine. Puffy clouds dotted the sky in silver hues, and the moon played coy games of hiding its beauty among its whispered enticeal. In and out it fled to secrecy, letting its living light dim in the waves of billowy softness — how sublime was the show. And ah now a coyote takes up his midnight serenade, letting his heart cry forth to please his love. No breeze to stir the air, just a living calmness, and a gentle sound of trickling water to give balance to the coyote's waning call of communion fulfilled.

For hours I lay embraced in the dark of silver shadows, listening to the sweetness of contemplative silence, and absorbing the warmth of water and life. How sweet, how sweet — this is the darkness of day that I know, and the night I long to share. It embraces those who step bravely into its arms, and gives wonders no less than the sun. So off I silently walk, letting its peace swallow my heart and whisper of wonder unknown.

Art Plate 2-58 ~ Darkness, of Polarity~

As the sun is made visible
by the unfathomable blackness,
wisdom is brought to light
by the vast darkness of ignorance
that engulfs it.
Can one exist
without relation to the other?
Is not the immensity of the void
given meaning by an object
resting within its embrace?
Light beckons your heart,
yet it is darkness
that opens the vision.
Your spirit sojourns amidst polarities,
that spring eternal in wayward reach,
but can they sustain?
And is infinity a trap
spirit unmercifully shuns?
Accept it all;
see the relationship
interwoven as its fabric,
even dance amidst its play of shadows,
as light forcasts
an illusion of perspective.
A dream needs relativity
to grasp unfathomable mysteries,
but why define
the edges of a miracle;
is it not enough to walk enfolded
in nights of future past,
and laugh at the wonder
that something blooms fragrant
out of the emptiness?
Yet the spirit is free,
singing on,
and its song creates worlds
of life unimaginable.
Oh how sublime is the dark light.

Art Plate 2-59 ~ Our Reflection

I walked into a house of mirrors, and everywhere I looked I saw myself reflected. My image brought relevance to the substance of the glass, and thus provided an avenue of relationship within the manifested realm of its illusory relativity. I could now relate a selfhood into the limiting factor of the mirror, but of what value would be gained by naming the illusory forms? would crying out 'this is myself number one, and that one myself number two,' give the illusion greater substance? Does keeping time within a dream lend greater relevancy to the fantasy? Does defining the spacial configuration of a shadow provide it a reality? Thus to name our reflection merely defines the limitation of our mind, and form is but a reflection of infinite expression in awareness of itself. We abide in a realm of mirrors, and how grand it is to laugh, but we need no limiting definitions to bind us into forgetfulness of what the true reality is; for the mirror and its reflection may be plays of illusory consciousness, but the perceiver is the eternal Self dancing in the shadows of eternity's light, and giving substance to Reality's play of Self awareness.

Art Plate 2-60 ~ Flowing Reflections ~

Reflected deep within our soul,
beyond a surface image
wavering with ripples of hopeful dreams,
a seed lies dormant
awaiting a nurturing rain,
patient beyond remembrance,
for it has never forgotten truth,
and awaits rebirth into expression.

Blinded by choice,
the mind recognizes only shadows
cast across a shallow sea,
as waves break tumultuous
upon a barren shore of faith,
yet heart reads the depths,
and knows of mystery unfathomable;
but communion is beyond
a clinging hope,
and still awaiting birth,
lying deep within recesses,
is an essence pure,
spiritual in light,
ungraspable in form;
yet reality has never presented itself,
and subtle flows the spirit,
hindered of current
by protruding masses of ego,
islands of desire,
alas whole continents of concepts —
where do we journey
that we need such profusion of clay?

Spirit is freedom
born into movement —
the stars in fascination
investigating the void,
wind swirling into joyous song,

water breathing in ebb and flow
to universal breath,
and here we plant roots,
discordant in stagnant concepts,
and wonder why spirit
lies dormant awaiting birth.

Impermanence is our name,
and joyous the flow of consciousness
when unbridled by fear.
Fear of what?
all is God,
spirit essence of eternal life,
flowing thru dreams,
and death but a concept
born of blindness,
as evolution
patiently explains the flow.

It all is flow,
and balanced in harmony,
for the Absolute is one whole,
and a totality must exist in equilibrium,
for what can throw
the 'One' out of balance?
So the 'One' flows
in the dream of the many,
yet nothing has changed but name,
and still deep within
the spirit awaits,
birth if it will,
or perhaps observing
a curious flow...

One Dream

Behold the Earth,
an obelisk
to the patience of time,
a monolith
floating in an uncharted sea.
Its writings carry no secret,
and its vision is blind,
yet its life is so mysterious.
Ghosts of consciousness
heralding the sun
live wrapped within its folds;
yet roam the clouds
where laughter carries their dream,
but cling in desire
for the foolish hope of form.
Forgetting the light
they wander in the dark,
walking circles
within their mind.

Perhaps we can remind them
of the dream,
and let the truth
dispel such shadows.
But who are we?
are we not also a dream,
foolishly watching the show,
claiming one vision
truer than another,
for who can say
which dream be true,
within the sacred soul
of the Dreamer.

Art Plate 2-61 ~ Primal Light ~

We stand at the edge
of a darkened chasm,
it is our forgetfulness
plummeting deep
into the bottomless abyss of ignorance,
but the dark is illusion.
There is a light radiant;
it is born in the awareness
of our Self,
and shines forth thru consciousness,
into manifest expression.
We reach across
a bridge of light,
and life blossoms into birth;
it is not separate
from the light divine,
it is the rays of its expression,
communicating eternal awareness.
And this be the relationship
we form to establish communion
within our Self.
We are here to share a light
born of purity,
a vision within
that expresses an outward sight.
A dream infinitely embraced,
echoing on thru eternity,
and lasting all but a moment.
And thus the oneness
breaths in awareness of itself,
eternal and sacred,
casting forth the primal light,
ever turning,
always burning.

Art Plate 2-62 ~ Heart Offering ~

And it made my heart soar
just to see him . . .

Once again life blooms into the light,
rising upon roots of love,
and nurtured by wisdom's tender embrace.
It is Mother springing eternal —
the hope born of awareness,
taking upon the wings of freedom,
beyond yet ever present.
The fragrance drifts upon the wind,
joyously the flower ever giving of itself;
it is union expanding its awareness,
and evolving past barriers,
and we so gently float
within the love of recognizing our source,
communion made possible only by birth;
but no loss does life suffer
in drifting into greater division,
for fragrance and flower
are lit from one essence,
and wind be their radiance of hope.
And could awareness ever be the loser?
one essence dreaming the two,
and watching the union it nurtures.
Fascinated? perhaps. Joyful? maybe.
And life continues to bloom
in Mother's eternal dance,
echoing thru eternity,
visions of a dream gone by —
captured by this moment,
and striking a call for the future.
Ah the truth, so simple in confusion,
but who is there to question a dream?
surely not the dreamer.
And on we laugh,
and on we spin,
dreaming, dreaming,
always dreaming . . .

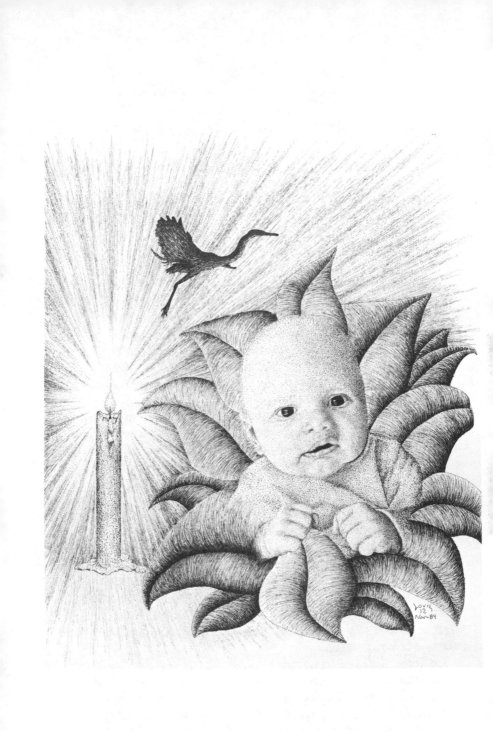

261

Wanderings of The Heart

Sawtooth Wilderness ~ August 1987 ~

How awesome are the Rockies, and the
Sierras are grand, but there are other
ranges of virgin heights that rival
their spectacular beauty, and one such
cluster of snow caped peaks is the
Sawtooth Mountains of Idaho. For a
week I walked its pristine grandeur,
but one day holds vivid a memory so
sublime. Though I ventured to most of
its lakes, and cut a trail across its
passes deep into its heart, the spot
that captured my soul was a hidden
area few ever are blessed to see, for
danger lies along this course, and few
have ever heard tales of its wonder—
I call this hidden gem "The Cathedral".

The sunrise found me walking amidst
the pines, rising into higher elevations.
My timing was right, for only during
brief times of the year will the hidden
valley of "The Cathedral" allow entrance
into its realm of glaciers, tarns and
jagged rocks. Up the rocky flank I cut
my course, following a deer trail to a
cleft where the snow melt sent a
cascading waterfall plummeting 300
feet into the chasm below. Loose rock
and tricky footwork brought keen
attention to the awareness of beauty
enfolding me.

Finally I reached the first lake within
the hanging valley that leads upward to
the glacier pathway. Goat lake is a
beautiful example of a gouged glacier
lake, carved out of solid granite and

surrounded by towering cliffs. A few hikers come to its shore to find solitude, but rarely do they continue up into the higher peaks. The highest crests of the sawtooth range surrounds this isolated spot, and from their flanks several glaciers have carved a bowl along its sheer base. It is very deceptive to the eye, and as I stood along the shore of Goat lakes transparent azure water, gazing at the glacier that dropped sheer into the lakes far end, it surely did not appear that another valley could possible lay above the glacier. It looked very much like the jagged peaks dropped straight into a narrow crevice where a stream and glacier emerged. But my curiosity is the door to most all my adventures, and I decided to climb the glacier for a better look.

The glacier was enormous, and took me an hour to scale its face, with many opportunities laying hidden to drop thru its ice to the freezing river flowing 50 feet below in its death, cold domain. Careful footing all the way, and keen concentration as to a possible course, but the crest of the glacier delivered to me an overwhelming surprise. As I rounded the top I found in front of me a winding cleft that opened into a hidden valley – not a straight valley, but a meandering wide gorge that rose in a series of waterfalls. It was a solid granite bowl, and behind each waterfall was a flat, depressed area of dozens of little tarns all connected together by an ice coated trickling creek. Rock outcroppings were everywhere, and on their crests were the

263

few trees that dotted this spectacle. The sides were sheer rock rising 2,500 feet to the awesome peaks above - with a few scattered trees clinging to the granite escarpments for precious life.

As I crossed one waterfall after another, and gazed upon the pools that filled each succeeding basin I came deeper into a communion with its heart, and felt a reverence build within me so as to instill the feeling that I was entering a sacred cathedral to offer up the prayer that is my life. Golden light filled its rarified air, and utter stillness added to the sanctum of its holy inspiration, much like a celestial choir ushering my way thru a corridor into my own soul.

I stopped to gaze in the pools, and to my surprise they had multi-colored algae covering the bottom. The edges of all the pools were lined with algae carpets of red, orange and yellow in every imaginable shape and hue, much as the fine weaving of a tapistry. It was dazzling to the eye, and adding to its effect, the higher ponds now had thick, lush carpets of green moss surrounding the pools. As I went ever higher the character of the bowl continuously changed, and soon the ponds formed into an icy, cascading creek that marched its way in silvery falls up to the peaks looming overhead. Now grass appeared in a few isolated spots, and gnarled pines rooted at their edges, and here I found a sanctuary to rest and gaze at the snow clad summits reaching far above me.

Captured within a miniture forest on the lushest carpet of grass, silence provided the only sound, and off a ways a silvery thread of cascading diamonds ran as icicles thru a granite crevice. Warmth from the sun to provide nurishment, and the crispest air to light my heart. A reverie of contemplative wonder filled my soul, and here in this miracle I was the conscious dream breathing life into a realm so pure — my heart could only in respect call this haven 'The Cathedral'.

As death marches to a drummer, and life rings of glories beheld, I would give them both a course to march the gallient parade, and let it be within the sacred walls of this cathedral. But here it is the heart that sees, and the eyes will have its time of wonder, but spirit echos between these walls guiding a course of inner remembrance. Perhaps I walked that day beyond the valley floor, and maybe the pools were not as glistening gems, or the peaks as azurine stretching to the sky. Maybe the air brought lightness to my head, and I walked dazed in a realm beyond; but I have journeyed the mountain crest for oh so many years, and my heart can feel when a place rings of truth. And thus it was that radiant day as the light glowed in tones of gold; the water ran pure, and the air sang serene, and I was one with its breath.

Art Plate 2-63 ~ Mood of a Dream ~

I am the mood
of the path I walk.
Beyond physical,
embraced in spirit,
communing in a dream.
Out of the mist of Reality
I sojourn into consciousness,
enfolded by shadow,
yet hold firm in remembrance,
though it be shroudded in fog
it gives freedom.
I feel the presence
of conscious awareness,
and relationship forms
thru this feeling,
becoming a symphony,
harmonic yet discordant.
My form is energy,
not graspable or contained,
and in its mystery
I watch reflections of myself;
it be the echo
sounding thru eternity,
deep in wonder,
yet the very fiber of life.
So on I walk
thru the reaches,
but I am not in them,
they are of me,
my sinew and strength;
and here I wander,
as the fog parts,
absorbed by the oneness,
expressing its serenity,
and ever walking,
always walking . . .

The Path Home

For how many weary years
have I walked this road to my house,
with eyes blind in future aspiration,
but never till today
did I see that another course
lay hidden in the trees.
Scarcely visible in a wooded glen
rests a lightly used diverging path,
and curiousity now raises my eyes,
or is it something I hear whispering.
But I know not where this trail leads,
and fear grips my mind,
but softly the whisper
speaks gentle in rhyme —
this forest is your home,
how far can you stray,
see what lies beyond that bend,
and at most lose but a day.
Though the path be rarely used,
straight and uncluttered be its way,
unlike the well traveled road
that weaves a winding course,
strewn with timber and rock.
Obviously few ever venture this path,
for the ground is soft,
and no dust marres the beauty
of this lively profussion of flowers.
Fragrance and song fill the air,
and peeking secretively animals follow,
as welcomed companions to adventure ;
but off ahead lay a meadow,
lush in springs velvety green,
and in it someone stands,
waiting in my path.
Fear brings panic to my mind,
yet tenderly the whisper still lingers,
urging me on toward my destiny.

Cautiously I step
with increasing apprehension,
and now the figure is easily seen.
The eyes are bright and fearlessly loving,
and I recognize something familiar.
Closer I come, and yes,
this man is one I know;
but he is not bent,
and no wrinkles cover his face,
and every pore exudes a strength,
but it must be so,
for I am sure,
that this man before me is me.
There I stand in power and peace,
on the path that bespeaks my freedom,
and the road I used
for so many years,
took me to a house estranged.
And on this simple path
buried deep in a forest fold,
I walk a day that never ends;
for after all these long and weary years
I finally have arrived home,
and there awaiting me was my self,
who so graciously bid me welcome,
and in compassion took me in.

Art Plate 2-64 ~ Stand Alone ~

Footprints scattered across the shore,
but I walk a beach untraveled.
A dying sun
speaks of my desire,
yet I embrace life
from afar.
I have not come
to follow the ignorance
of others,
or live by
their expectations.
My way lies
in following my heart,
and this course is one
few choose to follow.
But deterred I am not
if I must stand alone,
walking the shore in solitude.
Freedom brings peace,
not loneliness,
and the grace of Mother
flows in abundance
for those who stand
firm within their heart,
and let its whisper
dictate the course
their feet will wander.

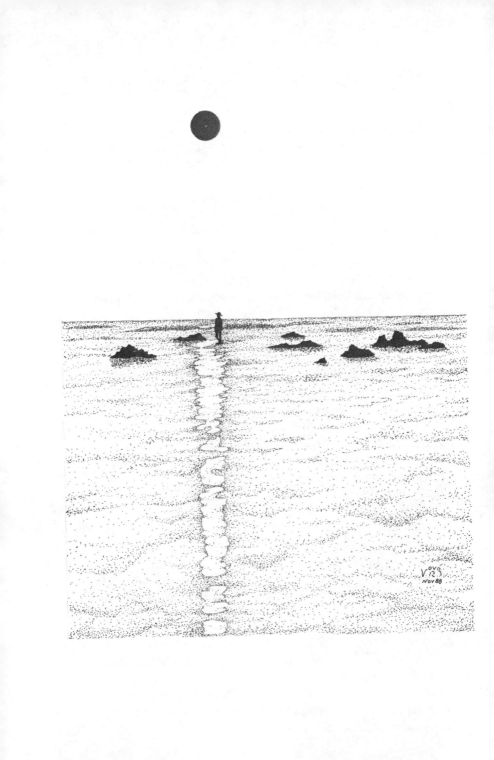

Remembrance of Sorrow

There is a soul stirred
from dreams untold,
and your laughter can be no deeper
than the longing it holds,
and tears have issued truth
throughout the ages of recollection.
But can sorrow be embraced
without tears of self pity?
Only when the soul cries forth,
stirred from a depth primeval,
longing to eternity to embrace our Cause,
and wearying of a sojourn
stretching unremembered,
past infinity, cloaked from our reach,
ever knowing purity lay beyond —
a dream in desperation
recapturing its dream,
and our course lay within its shadows.

But what of this moment,
does it carry no voice
to bespeak of its value,
that we cloud our eyes with tears
to blind us of its vision.
Is it not possible
that our remembrance
be no further away
than the breeze so gently caressing us?
does not the babbling brook carry a voice
to stir us from our slumber?
We are in the midst of an orchestration
bent on capturing our attention,
for all these tears of remembrance,
are but echos
confusing us into forgetfulness.
Perhaps both laughter and sorrow
are the illusory maze

we so desperately long to escape,
and in despair we have watched this play
for so very long.

Yet all eternity dances on,
and still we wander from our refuge,
while we forlornly look and weep.
Our only chains are our involvement
beyond our capacity to love,
for in purity,
we need not forge an anchor of emotion
to bind us to desire.
This moment explains itself,
if we but listen to its whisper
with a heart of innocence.
We have built castles
to protect a flimsy lump of clay,
and let our spirit roam
in the tattered clothes of a begger;
sinking roots deep
into a soil of impermanence,
and there we stagnate,
anchored as a tree,
tearfully viewing our lost heritage.

But can freedom be raped
and hidden from our hearts?
is it not the very air we breathe?
It is we who willingly trade
the crisp mountain reaches,
for the foul air of our stagnant desires,
and hold ourself lifeless as a corpse
within the concepts of our frail longings.
Who told us that we where weak?
where did this timidness arise from?
We must not peak in fear
at a world built of strength,
and thus feel the stab of sorrow
of a communion given away.
Your fiber is the very Earth itself,

for it echos the power of your heart;
spirit be the foundation of this realm,
and you are the mystery
that has brought forth its call.

You are the miracle the ages have heralded,
with lineage direct to the soul of God.
If longing has the feel of separation,
it is only within the tears
that blind your heart into forgetfulness,
for our very essence
is the breath of creation,
and we have senses to touch this dream,
and commune with the power
that holds us within its embrace of love.
All existence confirms this moment,
and nowhere need we wander,
or need we search down
the corridors of desire,
to find the reality we are witness to.
We are the call primeval,
and our footsteps are the path
to witness the truth of life,
for though a dream weaves a tapistry
to sustain the souls fragile thread,
it is freedom's warning whisper
that webs of desire are also being woven,
by the weaver's tempting hand
amidst the paradox of illusion and faith.

The gentle call of freedom
can stir the heart to longing,
giving sorrow a hand to blind the moment,
for the roots of limitation are sunk firm,
and we have tears as companions
instead of stars.
We are the consciousness of awareness,
and destiny lies in a solitary walk
within the forrest of our soul.
And here deep in the recesses of evolution

freedom springs eternal as onward path,
and spirit finds choice within its traverse;
and only in its embrace
will the tears of sorrow,
and the longing for lost remembrances,
be cast from our course,
as boulders strewn to block the way.
We have placed them there ourself
throughout the ages,
covering the land with their shadows,
and how fearful our heart has become,
at the grotesque sight of the jagged plain.
But our view is one of perspective,
for we look from the belly of a worm.
Sincerity is the ground to stand upon,
and in humility recognize who you are,
as living awareness of God in reality,
and in this embrace of truth,
breath and height expand its view,
opening communion beyond limitation,
showing the jagged plain as it is —
rolling grains upon a sandy shore,
longing for your presence
as the very essence that brings it life.
Step forth into this light,
and let the waves beckon you on;
the way has always been guided
by a radiance issuing forth from yourself,
but blinded by desire you knew it not.
You are the sacred life
brought into existence
as consciousness of a supreme Reality,
and this eternal light is your true Self,
for death exists only
in concepts of clay,
and all eternity
you shall be that pure Reality,
for only one essence
fills this universe of dreams,
and forever we are that God...

Wanderings of The Heart

Disappointment Creek ~ Aug. 1986 ~

The Lizard Head wilderness treated me superbly, but now the canyons of Utah were issuing a welcoming cry. The peaks of colorado are wondrous, and how dearly I love the abundance of animal life and flowers, but Sept. and Oct. are a magical time for me, and the canyons of Utah are the epitome of power, so each year I try to combine the two, and thus walk blessed in a realm of miracle.

So off I headed on the dirt roads of western colorado, and here fate led me down an unknown valley. It is a large valley stretching on and on, but about mid way I came upon an area where there were large golden bluffs cast within 1000 foot vermillion cliffs set apart by twisting volcanic canyons of real amazing colors. So I decided to make home along this pea green colored creek called Disappointment, and hike to the bluff and thru the arroyos.

Ever winding the gully slowly brought me to the gold colored mesa, which surrounded the towering bluffs. As I popped up onto the lava strewn field I saw grazing a 100 feet before me a jet black stallion. He didn't see me, for I was partially hidden by an oak tree, so I stood frozen and watched him in delight. No fences or ranches have tamed this area, and stallions still run free and wild, and by the majestic, powerful build I could just feel his dominance over his desert domain.

Finally it was time to continue on, and I tried to slowly move below the ridge so as not to disturb him. But he spotted me at my first move, and peered intently at me as I held motionless once again. Obviously he was disturbed at my presence, and he began to look all about and then pranced back and forth lifting his front hooves real high while his mane and tail flew in the wind. He purposely came at an angle toward me, but stopped about 50 feet away, and then exhibited a most incredible display of pure animal power. I felt he was directly challenging me to battle as if I were another stallion, for not only did he lay down a stud pile, but he took up the most exaggerated performance of prancing I've ever seen. He galloped back and forth with his mane flying and tail erect as he wrangled his hooves in the air and let out his challenging cry. His display was utterly spellbinding, and I walked into the open field and stood in defiance to his show. But I was very curious why he was so agitated when I offered no threat. So I began to survey the area closely and the answer came quickly; on the ridge behind me was a pretty, little mare, and I innocently stood between the two of them. Well I'm no homewrecker, so I angled my walk to one side and he caught the hint and went running to the other side of the field, while the mare ran down the gulley and up behind the stallion. Now he was back in controlling position, and once again he started prancing, I guess just incase I changed my mind and decided to fight him, but I wished them farewell and sent my love to this wild lord of the prairie, and off they ran as the wind.

Continuing up the sloping field I started to enter into an area of giant, black lava boulders strewn across the base of the pure gold colored bluff. Big grey clouds began to cover the sun, and soon lightening was flashing around me, giving a primordial atmosphere that dinosaurs were lurking. When the rain joined the show, I quickly found a cozy home inside one of the hollowed lava boulders. Warm and dry I waited out the sudden fury and soon it subsided into a glorious array of colors, as rainbows softly painted a dream. Off I went from my hobbit cave up the steep flank of the bluff, now deeply colored gold from the showers. Toward the top, large red streaks added a touch of brilliance to the castle like formations that formed its crest. Large, hollowed out sandstone boulders and caves ringed the top, with twisted, gnarled pines holding onto the rocks for dear life. Exploring its small mesa top I found a golden cave hollowed with arches, and nestled into its cocoon warmth for a nap.

From my lofty perch I could see that there was a series of cliffs separated by twisting, black lava canyons leading to a high plateau that was protected by 1,500 foot red cliffs. One cliff area seemed to have a hanging valley of pines within it, and its intriguing nature invited me to challenge. Down the gold bluff and into the twisting labyrinth of arroyos I went. I've never seen such exaggerated winding canyons as these, just to go about 2 miles I had to walk at least 5 miles back and forth and around in its maze of black and red volcanic canyons.

I finally did arrive at the cliffs, and pure, deep red signaled a complete change of terrain. Now pines and deep, steep ridges towered their way up 1000 foot cliffs. The hanging valley was really a depressed part of the sloping cliff, but I decided to climb one its gully systems to see the overall view of the bowl formed within the cliffs, and also the maze I crossed that stretched to the gold bluff. The gully was steep, and after gaining about 400 feet in elevation it turned into part of the cliff, but the view was partly blocked by the gullies walls; so I decided to climb from the bottom of the gorge to the ridge that made up its walls. It was only an added 100 feet in height, but it provided a really grand view of the unusual character of these cliffs.

Instead of descending back to the gully to return downward, I decided to just go down the ridge and hope I could get off it somewhere. The ridge stayed consistently about 100 feet above the gully bottom, and it was easy going down it, and best of all I received great views the whole way; but with still a little ways to go I reached an area of giant pillars protruding out of the ridges backbone. I was now sort of stuck, for I couldn't get around the pillars, and I didn't want to walk all the way back up the ridge, and I was 100 feet above the gully, and it was far to steep to climb down. So I decided to try a risky manuver by attempting to go around the pillars on the side of the cliff, and carve footsteps into the rocky soil as I went. I only had to traverse 30 feet, so I figured it wouldn't be too difficult.

The first few steps I carved were straight down till I was below the pillars by 5 feet, then I started to cross horizontal, but a funny thing happened; the ground had been soft enough to carve for the first few steps, but all at once the ground became hard as rock and wouldn't carve at all, and since my first two downward steps would not allow me to reverse them in an upward direction, I now stood on a very precarious cliff 100 feet above a rock strewn gorge, and was sort of trapped. Well I could have figured something out if I had a little time, but as I stood gripping the loose rocky soil fate decided to raise its fickled head and have it rain. I felt a few drops and then it began to come in earnest, I now had no time to ponder my predicament, and it was indeed a serious one. I had been holding on with great difficulty when the soil was dry, and now the rocky soil was getting wet and my weight was causing it to break away. What to do? I had to act quick, or within a minute I would fall to my death. I didn't have time to try to recarve my previous steps, and I couldn't go up or down, and the soil was washing away rapidly from under my feet. I was starting to slip when I heard a voice within me clearly say, "run down the cliff". I twisted my head to look at the steep cliff and the jagged boulders a 100 feet below, and sort of sighed in despair as I continued to slip. And then the same voice said, "run down the cliff", but this time it spoke with such incredible authority and urgency that I immediately let go of the wet rock, twisted around, and stepped out into space.

I am no novice or fool when it comes to danger in the wilderness, and I kept my head as I quickly surveyed the death course that lay below me. I sort of slid and leaped as I plummeted down the cliff, but I saw that little 3 inch deep rain grooves covered the side of the cliff, and about the width of my boot. So I jammed my boot into the depression and twisted my foot to lock it in and slow me down, and then I quickly released and pushed off to another depression, while at the same time I reached for any little bush or twig to grab. With my hands on every shrub in reach, and my feet twisting into the rain slots I was able to run down the cliff, or said more accurately I sort of fell with control. It all happened very rapidly and I focused my eyes on where I wanted to hit, and had my feet running so I would land and somersalt. It was crazy, but the voice must have been guiding me also, for I ran down the cliff breaking my fall and spun as I hit; and the next thing I knew I was standing on my feet looking up to where I had been, as water ran down the cliff, and I wasn't noticeably hurt, just a few scratches. I just shook my head in disbelief, and then in sincerity I gave thanks to the power that is our life.

The rain stopped shortly after I descended, and beautiful puffy clouds filled the sky. I didn't want to repeat the meandering thru the maze, so I ascended its backbone and walked up and down its black sand, pyramid ridge. How grand to look down to the catacombs of twisting rock, and behind me lay the red cliffs of earth that blessed me with a glimpse of my death. Before me stretched the golden bluff where I was challenged to live in raw awareness. A thousand years elapsed in a day, and could not have displayed greater power and abundance of adventure.

I start each hike with no expectation, and let the challenge unfold as it may. Some days I walk on the gentleness of grace, and others there is a challenge of death awaiting, and in freedom I am prepared for all occasions. Because I am on friendly terms with my death, I also am blessed with a joyous communion with life. I cling or grab at neither, but walk respectfully within the truth of my spiritual nature, thus a grand play goes on around me, while I resist from dictating terms of its unfoldment. Life is its own explanation, and acceptance brings remembrance of the truth of my soul. Thus I merely watch and react as my heart leads the way, and where my path will lead is of no great concern.

Art Plate 2-65 ~ Power ~

Art Plate 2-66 ~ One Dream ~

Born upon the wings of power,
life streams into the light
of consciousness,
ever expanding into a void
that fills the space of time.
Clay is not our home,
it is but fabric
to weave relationship within ourself.
There is but one power,
resting in activity of its awareness,
dreaming forth the infinite,
eternally at wonder within its recognition;
for we be the soul
yearning of communion,
casting visions within our heart,
melting into the oneness.
The dream encompasses the dreamer,
and our essence is pure,
a reality beyond illusions of clay;
and breath is our union,
right its vehicle,
to bring remembrance
of visions internal.
The eyes speak
of mysteries know and forgotten,
yet shadows cannot blind the truth;
our spirit shines eternal
in union with awareness absolute,
for in repose,
does not our mind
spin plays mysterious and strange,
as above so below;
and thus the dream
dreams its dream,
and forgets about the dreamer.

Something by itself is obvious —
        only the Absolute 'is'...

Wanderings of The Heart

Thousand Lakes Wilderness ~ Aug. 1985~

My life is lived in raw challenge, and for the last 5 years its direction has been guided by an inner voice. Clearly audible within my senses, it has delivered me from many a precarious spot, but yet this whisper of my inner spirit, or better yet Mother's guiding light, is the very calling breath that has caused all my adventures where death reaches its embrace. So the echo resounds, and I know its dictates, and now so willingly I follow in anticipation of the light of wisdom so often gained. But how many years I reluctantly questioned a voice intuitively speaking from my heart, so the lessons were slow, yet poignant in delivery, and now I can look upon the panorama, and recall Mother's guiding hand so lovingly pushing me beyond my selfhood toward freedom.

Sometimes it is necessary to test one's blind faith, and find if purity of heart overrules the ego's clinging to relativity— a demonstration where death watches to see if will-power overrules common sense. My hike took me into the heart of Thousand Lakes Wilderness, and its highest peaks were my call. No problems presented themselves as I climbed the ridge that held its highest crests. Each held a magnificent view, with Mt. Shasta and Mt. Lassen dominating this lava encrusted area, separated by dense patches of thickly forested pines. Funny they should name it thousand lakes when

from atop its highest peak I could count
but eight little lakes.

Departing the main ridge I descended
into the lava bowl below, and rising
directly ahead was a red lava cliff
towering upward to another high ridge of
volcanic peaks. My course should have
taken me southward to circumvent the
cliffs, where an easy access up a talus
slope would deliver the ridge in short
time. But ah that inner voice rose
clearly and announced to my bewildered
surprise that I should climb directly up
its vertical cliff. I was reluctant, but
hesitantly I approached the base of the
lava escarpment to survey its difficulty.

I am not a technical rock climber,
but I do have some skill, but what
rose verticle for 300 feet in front of me
was a nightmere bent for suicide. It
wasn't really rock, and there was no
stability to its form — what the cliff
consisted of was volcanic sand pushed
together by pressure, but crumbled apart
with the slightest touch. A few larger
boulders protruded here and there, but
the face was riddled with small water
shoots that carved this course, rocky
sand into jagged edged reliefs. At the
base of the cliff was a huge pile of
fine sand that presented a considerable
amount of difficulty just to walk thru,
but to actually attempt to climb this
moving avalanche of lava dust seemed
unthinkable. And thus the test was
presented, to go beyond thought into a
presence of power where action dictates
survival of spirit, and where death of
body is inconsequential.

The first 50 feet found me strong

enough to overpower the sliding sand, using my entire body to friction up the cliff. Arms, legs, stomach and chest were pressed against the lava to provide leverage, and each knob was indeed a welcomed sight. But strength slowly waned, and fortitude replaced it with subtle technique. After 100 feet of height was gained, the straight drop extracted a price in courage, and now unbending intent was guide to my suicidal assult. A small depressed gully added another 100 feet closer to the rim, and perhaps I could use it to gain the summit. Yes, it continued on, and even added a small margin of safety, although its sandy rock was the loosest yet, and crumbled to sand beneath my feet. Now only 20 feet till I reached the top, but oh my, an overhanging cliff guarded its crest, like the formidable fortress of a castle.

This sandy, lava cliff was nearly impossible to climb upward, so I couldn't imagine trying to climb downward, better to jump and sing to a quicker death. So up I inched, and using my hands I broke rock loose from the cliff to give me a course upward. Inch by inch I crawled, using all my strength to push my belly against the loose rock to gain precious friction. But how to pull myself over the top when there was nothing but loose sand to grab? Ha, what a play of tricks — one after another, but each one solveable with total focused awareness and no superfluous thought; intuition was the guide here, and delivered avenues of escape to each trap it set.

As the final joke, after I did manage to struggle my way over the brim and stand upon its sacred red crest, it proved to be a totally meaningless climb, for not only was the view minor, but a trail led across the ridge of this crest. But this play had nothing to do with yodeling mountaineering, it was a test of faith over physical consciousness. Spiritual realization is a recognition of Reality, yet words prove little in this domain; only demonstration brings faith into dominance, and in the final analysis it proves to be the only way to grasp your knowledge as power, and prove the truth of your spiritual reality to yourself.

For years now I have lived in this faith, letting challenge prove its reality, but my first years of spiritual sojourn did not carry this conviction, and only by grace was I given concrete examples of Mother's encompassing reality. Though Mother now speaks thru an inner voice, which I attentively always listen for, the first time I was to receive the blessing of her compassionate light, it was much more of a physical demonstration.

Winter of 1981 found me on the coast of Big Sur climbing the cliffs, as the high tide pounded the bluffs. I had come to an area where the cliffs fell straight into the sea at least 50 feet in vertical sheerness. But further out into the water the cliff receded to about 25 vertical feet. So there I stood on the rock strewn shore debating my course. If I wished to proceed further along the bluffs, I would have to wait for a low section of waves, and then run quickly across the highest protruding points of slick boulders sticking out of the water, and jump onto the face of the cliff at

its shortest point, and quickly climb to the
top before a wave crashed into me. I
pondered the timing and looked diligently
for a route on the cliff, but I couldn't
see the holds well enough from where I
stood on the beach, and it just didn't
seem I would have enough time between
waves to pull it off. But being rather
young and intelligently foolish, I made
a mad dash to test my courage. I made
it across the kelp strewn boulders, and
managed to leap onto the cliff, but now
I was disoriented as to where I remembered
a possible course up the cliff.

I got about half way when I came to
an area of black, wet, slick rock that was
smooth as glass. I was ready to start
pondering my course, as I clung with
toes griping the vertical cliff and
fingers dug into little holes, when I
heard a horrible sound, and turning my
head toward the breakers, here came a
monster wave. It was real close too,
and in a matter of seconds it would
rip me off the wall and dash me into
the rock boulders below, and then
pound on me with all its force. Death's
arrival but two seconds away doesn't
give one alot of time to ponder a
technical rock course up an impossible
cliff. There was a jutting rock up 4 or
5 feet above me, but it was out of
reach; I needed one hold inbetween to
allow me to stretch up to it and pull
me to safety. But what to do, nothing
was there to grasp on this glassy, slick
rock. One second and then death, and
now the moment of truth — I yelled
out "Mother save me", and threw my
hand upward toward the slick area of

290

glassy rock. By letting go of my hold I should have fallen, as the wave crashed upon me, but instead I felt a distinct pressure, similar to a hand, grab my wrist and hold it; so quickly I threw my other arm up, and pivoted on the wrist being held, and stretching, I managed to grab the jutting rock above, and pull myself upward as the wave hit at my feet, crashing its way to the shore.

I was safe and had only a few feet to go to reach the top of the cliff, but before I went further, my doubting curiosity had to be appeased. I looked back to where I had reached up into the smooth area and hung on to something, but sure enough the surface was slick and glassy, and there was no possible way I could have grabbed anything physical. My wrist was indeed held, and long enough for me to save myself, and just recalling this tremendous gift of Mother's grace brings on overwhelming thankfulness, and has been a continual source of inspiration and guidance. For years that episode proved itself a foundation to build upon, as a firm reminder of the spiritual reality that is our life, beyond the physical appearance of relative existence. I never made it a prayer to ask for proof or demonstration, but I did continuously beseech Mother to graciously appear and quench my spiritual thirst with her living presence.

A new seven year cycle began, and now I traveled north this May of 1984, stopping to meditate in the serenity of a secluded cove at Salt Point State

Park. Upon a picnic table I layed out my meditation carpet, and sat in a half lotus posture gazing out upon the waves gently breaking on the cliffs below me. Above the water by 50 feet, I was enfolded between pines and a rocky outcropping that dropped as an over-hanging cliff into the breakers. Though the wind had a steady force, it only gently caressed me, being sheltered within the cove. In meditative silence I drew inward, yet kept my eyes open to the beauty of crashing waves and the prismatic colors of a burgeoning sunset.

Quietly I heard footsteps from behind, and then passing by, one by one, a dozen gentle souls walked to the rock outcropping and stood close together gazing upon the sea, as a celestial choir awaiting their leader to guide them in reverant song. And lo that leader now arrived; ever so quietly a radiant woman approached the rock cliff and stood upon its furthest jutting point, like a finger of stone it reached to the beckoning waves, and there she stood at the very brink with her back to the ocean, and now spoke to the group so attentively gazing upon her. Radiantly she glowed of peace, but the waves kept me from hearing her words. Ten minutes past by as a second, captivated by the powerful energy I felt. Then the silent group once again passed my way, but as each approached me they bowed and smiled sweetly, and continued out of my sight.

But the woman stayed, now turning

toward the ocean with outstretched arms,
beckoning and blessing, and staying
in a communion of prayer for a time
that only love can measure. Then the
wonder of it happened; she walked
over to me and stood before me, and
we melted into each others eyes – time
passed, yet frozen by eternity, I know
not for how long. Then a cascade of
tears began to flow down her face
falling in huge drops upon the ground,
and I knew if I could but catch one
of those precious teardrops I would
hold all the secrets of this vast
universe. But firmly I was held in
meditative arms and could not move.
She then lifted her hand and placed
it on my cheek and radiantly lit with
a light of pure love, which I echoed
back to reflect the blossoming of our
communion. She spoke to me soft
and pure as she tenderly stroked my
cheek, and the words still ring in
crystal clarity, and I knew in my
heart that Mother was indeed blessing
me with the gracious gift of her
presence, a gesture of love to my
continual plea. Unreserved my love
flowed out, yet I could not move from
my rigid posture, as if held firm
between two worlds, where earth cast
chains upon my spirit.
Ever so sadly the blessing ended,
for eternity cannot be held stagnant
upon a tear, and Mother now softly
walked away, but I could not turn to
see where she went, and after a few
steps I heard no sound, as if she be
swallowed by eternity's embrace,
leaving only the sweetness of fragrance

as trace of her love.

Vividly I recall those moments of
heart communion, and forever will
they be etched as epitaph to a doubting
mind ; ah, but my heart always
knew of the truth, and by Mother's
grace I captured it as a staff to bear
me thru a wandering journey upon
the thread of life's denial. For I am
a spiritual being, born of living love,
the awareness of one Reality ; and my
life is the dedication of remembrance
to this truth, and so I walk, and
so I fly, and challenge is my freedom.

Remembrance

How joyous are these days
of unclouded remembrance,
contented of heart
in the feeling & serenely watch.
Sun blazing in fluorescent hues,
its dying embers
beckoning a fiery death.
Shadows rising into a blackening canopy,
bringing utter stillness,
broken only by a cricket's call.
Specks flashing in the dark,
etching figures to raise curiousity
of worlds cloaked in mystery untold.
Thought escapes this time of peace,
as the moment accepts its life,
bestowing eternity
into precious remembrance,
as the sea tranquilly
subdues its waves.
Nothing can be added
when the heart makes no demands,
and insight is not needed
if the mind has no where to dwell.
How can the past capture me
if it has no voice,
and where can the future lie
when all desire stands aside.
Joyous is this reverie
nurtured in sweet remembrance,
for I have loosed my bonds,
and did I ever forget?

Dream of My Waking

I laughed a thousand years ago,
and still I wait for the echo.
Oh, if I could only grasp it all,
but that is just the dream of a child.
Eternity sings
with the voice of discovery,
yet still I walk this mystery alone.
Each flower holds the wonder
of the ages,
and issues a challenge to the heart.
Where are the eyes
to behold the rainbow,
and ears to hear the crashing waves?
Surely others dance in the rain,
and gently caress this earth.
Are they swallowed
within its rapturous folds,
hidden by the heart of their longing?
The peaks are bare,
the canyons empty,
where do these brave souls wander?
I've looked all of eternity,
and yet no reflections have I crossed.

Perhaps when this dream is forgotten,
and shadows linger no more,
I will look upon a valley pure,
where crystalline waves
flow to the sea,
and boughs sway
to a gentle breeze.
Perhaps the grass
will glisten with dew,
and hues of red and gold
embroider the leaves.
I'll walk along
a murmuring brook,

encouraging the fish
to dart and leap ;
and here a rare soul
will dwell in peace,
ignorant of their wisdom.
Laughter will be the only words,
and a smile the bonding of our hearts.
How simple it is to walk,
amidst the song of birds.
The sun be warm,
and the air is free,
and the breeze caresses me in love.
No days will pass,
but time will wane,
and strength will build a gate,
for two can sojourn
in freedom as one,
when there is nowhere to go.

With nothing to do,
all is a dream,
and who is to say
that two cannot dream
the same dream of the One.

Art Plate 2-67 ~ So Many Years ~

How many years ago
was I sitting upon my grave
pondering the mystery of death?
And for how long
have I tried to recapture
the memory of my youth?
It is but the desperation
of idle thoughts,
spinning emotions of time,
yet oh how they seem
to hold life itself.
How can I be pulled
by such a fragile thread?
If I ever would have understood
how tightly this web bound me,
perhaps I would have controlled
these wild steeds of the wind.

Now it seems much to late,
to reorder a century
of useless pondering,
and yet am I not this moment
reshaping the destiny
I now control,
or is this yet another consuming play?
Perhaps not,
for this time I feel
a turning of the leaves.
Could it be my heart that speaks
of a memory beyond my youth?
Perhaps my spirit
longs to be recaptured,
or have I ever allowed it life
within this corpse of useless thought.

What stirs within me
that now says I cannot die,

and that my grave
is but a keeper of time,
marking the movement of my soul.
I have exhausted this body
looking back in Death's memory,
and now I must visit with Life.
Oh how I've wasted
these precious years
trying to recapture dead thoughts.
There is no fool
like a dead fool,
and today my heart yearns to live,
and be exactly what I am.

And though my thoughts
will never fathom the depths,
my heart has always been there,
and at long last
it is time for silence,
and remembering
what I never forgot.

Eternity is a Long Time To Dream

Caught within a grasp
& curiously embrace,
the world throbs within my hand
slipping into eternity's oblivion.
Oh how time fleets away,
this kaleidoscope of swirling vision,
for just now I closed my eyes,
only a brief instant of wayward breath,
to drink the potent brew
of a meditative bliss,
and behold! alreddy ten years
have slipped away,
lost to a doubting memory.
Each moment of silent communion
has the world recede
further into shadows of illusion,
painting dreams upon my dream,
but I am here,
always here,
watching where I was.
My heart sings free,
but the mind
uselessly clings to its song,
a clever irony that binds it is desire,
yet my spirit rejoices in the echo.
Consciousness I be
of the reflection I see,
as laughter diffuses the light.
So on I sit
and serenely observe,
watching fascinated by paradox blatant,
held in love so subtle;
but this day will not last,
for I be the perpetual dreamer,
and once again
I will close my eyes,
and the years will slip away
uncounted ...

I have scaled the peaks of relativity to gain understanding and knowledge. But as I stand gazing into the complexity of unimagineable vastness, I hear the laughter of time. Where have I come from, that I find a need to search? Do I spin webs to cover the simplicity of the truth? Laughter rings thru the valley, yet I heard it not as I scaled the peaks; was I deaf and blind to the very path I walked? So now I stand empty and begin again, knowing that my knowledge has no value. Opening my arms to my ignorance, I stand bare and allow my consciousness to be embraced by that which a selfhood could not acknowledge. I find that I am that one essence of which my path was made; ah the paradox, for I am the very ground I walk and the mountain I stand upon. The laughter is internal, for I have laughed all of eternity, knowing that I am the one reality, and playing the game of watching myself walk within my dream. Oh what joy it is to remember my dance of freedom, and commune as I watch the play. So now I stand in the serenity of my heart, and truly can I laugh with all the voices of consciousness.

303

Wanderings of The Heart

Needles Overlook, Utah ~Sept. 1984~

Can a book contain the joy of life, if it has no depth of sorrow, and yes even death, held within its covers. For five years I have buried the secret of my evolution to mastery, and now time points the way to speak about death of life, and birth of spirit. Never I felt would I share this episode, but these pages are not just a book exterior, but a chronicle within the hidden archives of my heart; and to rise into lighter realms and grow beyond limitation to ultimate freedom, I must release all clinging to form, and this book is vehicle to unburden my heart, and scatter its seeds to the wind. Forward I softly walk, and lighter the way becomes, so now the time has arrived to release all, and finally tell the epic of my death, and let it stand as testament to a new breath.

There is a spot nestled in the junipers, at the very brink of a 1,000 foot cliff, that looks down upon the twisted maze of canyonlands, some 3,000 feet below. Apart from where others venture, I have found an isolated place as kingdom to my heart, for it has always brought great strength and growth, and nurtured my body to further challenge. I can only give the greatest honor to its beauty unsurpassed, for upon its jagged ridge of red rock I stumbled upon my death.

Sunny, warm and a gentle breeze was the cocoon that guided my feet as I hiked upon the cliffs, and this day my course lay to the east guided by a morning sun. Pines and junipers cling bravely to the rock, and the soil is deep red sand. Life is scarce here, but deer and rabbits travel in secret, leaving prints to tell the tale. A week I had now walked the cliffs, and vaguely I can recall the first day that I had indeed seen two deer, but so odd was their behavior. One ran as I approached, but stopped as if waiting for the other—odd indeed for deer. And the other was a distance off, yet it didn't run, but slowly walked a ways and stopped; and even stranger it appeared to have a red bandanna around its neck, but the distance was too great, and perhaps my eyes deceived me, and I continued on without surveying them closer or giving much thought to this odd encounter.

But that was five days ago, and today I walk in joy east, climbing as an ant among the giant red boulders, and looking upon the incredible panorama that stretched to four mountain ranges carved deep by the Colorado river, a grand etching of 8,000 feet into the ancient seabed of years forlorn.

I crossed into a small depression held private by surrounding boulders and trees, a perfect secluded cove held sacred from wind and intrusion. Quietly I walked across its ground, and then a noise behind me. Turning quickly I was amazed and overjoyed to see a deer standing but five feet away. A loving smile lit my face to express my gratitude, but ever so quickly my smile was replaced by horror. Tears flowed as my legs buckled, and down to my knees I fell, crying out "Oh my God",

and openly weeping at the sight I beheld.
Yes, a deer did stand before me, and oh
yes how I love them so, but this
precious creature of love was so
desperately injured, for someone had shot
the deer, and blown its face to pieces.
Now I recalled the deer with the red
bandanna, but cloth it was not, this
poor creature had its jaw entirely
severed away, as it hung from a dried
bloody muscle. But how could 5 days
elapse? how could it continue to live in
suffering so long. Its jaw was shattered,
taking a direct shot to the face, but its
eyes were untouched, as it pitifully
looked at me, too weak to move. On
my knees I watched in tearful
compassion, as the deer stood wobbling
with its knees buckling in fatigue. No
food and loss of blood, and yes the
agony of five suffering days, had left
it a skeleton of shaking bones.
    Quickly I gathered my strength and
asked Mother for guidance; I had to
pull myself together and help my sister
of spirit. Standing I went to her side,
and no movement could she muster.
Gently I caressed her head to show my
loving intentions, and then I looked to
where she had lain, and thought it
best to lay her back within her hidden
bed. Though she was bigger than I, I
gently nestled my arms around her to
pick her up and carry her, but oh she
let out the most pitiful cry, feeling I
would harm her; it was the last noise
she ever made, and oh how it tore my
heart, and once again brought on a
blow of tears.
    With tears blinding my vision I

did pick her up, telling her of my love, and it did quiet her; then carrying her, I gently layed her in her deathbed and tried to make her at comfort. I wrapped my shirt around her and a cloth for a pillow, but oh how sad, she couldn't put her head down, for her nose had been torn apart, and she had to hold her head up, straining her neck just to awkwardly breathe in loud gasps.

I had to help her, and my heart spoke of her needs – warmth, food, water and then to a veterinarian. So off I ran, breaking all world records, back to my van – into my knapsack went lettuce, water and blanket, and then like the wind I raced back to my deer. I had told her I would return quickly, and departing had been painful, but I knew it was best, and now I brought with me new life to save its precious breath. I knelt down before her with new hope, and looked into her eyes as if to tell her that help was coming. But tears flowed once again as I saw the foolishness of my heart's blinded vision. This poor creature had no mouth left for which to eat and drink, and its eyes spoke of imminent death. My race was useless, and once again I asked for spiritual guidance as to what I must do. Not much time remained in the deer's life, so I cleared away my junk and sat by her side, leaving tears behind and raising all the strength I had to speak with love to its dying ears.

Softly I told my deer of its Godhood, and of the wonders of existence, and where its true reality lay. Quietly I spoke and soothed its fear of dying, while I caressed her and stroked her face. She became very calm and eased her muscles to relax into the words I spoke. Continuously flowing I soothed her with my love, and spoke of her spiritual life to be, assuring that death was her release into greater abundance of life. But some words of wishful peace slipped in, as I told her she would be having wings now like a divine Pegasus, and called her my Pegadeer, and promised that she would be living in a lush paradise eating celestial grass with other pegadeers. But mostly I spoke of God, and called her a divine light, telling her how beautiful she was. Only once did I break my strength and cried out softly, "Oh what they've done to you", but this brought an immediate and pronounced agitation from her that startled me, and I quickly composed myself and once again spoke of God, and she calmed immediately into peace.

Hours went by and her life slowly waned; breath became coarser and further spread – 15 seconds apart, then 30 seconds. I continued to talk softly, and she was at peace as I caressed her – now a minute apart; was there to be another breath? I anxiously awaited each breath, watching her eyes intently – yes, one more breath, now quiet – yet again one more. But ever so gently the luster of her eyes faded and opaque dullness set in, and with it death – there is no mistaking when the soul departs, for the eyes are its light, and vision but its dream.

But yet I continued to talk for

awhile longer, wishing a journey of
union with her source, and sending
love in hope of guidance to her
unfoldment into rebirth of spirit. My
tears flowed, for deep within me I
understood that this drama of death
that had unfolded was in fact my
own release from life. When her eyes
faded my life also departed, leaving
its wandering course of forgetful
ignorance, to be reborn into spiritual
remembrance. But still the form clung,
and with it a desire for life, yet its
strength was waning without the
heart's guiding support.

For hours I stayed by Pegadeer and
kept the flies away, but finally the
sun was setting, and I offered up my
tears to its dying light, and it also
spoke of death. Stumbling along I
managed to find my vehicle, and there
I sat dazed and wounded. Four days
went by as I shunned food, water and
sleep, being comforted only by tears,
and my selfhood cried forth its life,
drowned unto death within its grief.
I was in a daze deeper than life's
embrace, and slowly I died to the last
vestiage of my desire that lay hidden
in my form.

Emptied of all life I sat held together
by threads from a web I knew nothing
of. The luster of desire left my eyes
and death embraced my body, but ah
the paradox, for death was herald to
irony's touch. Death brought the gift
of life, and bestowed the grace of
Mother's breath, and once again I
breathed with life, and new luster
came to my vision. A physical death

to a spiritual birth, yet I was still empty, as a vessel waiting to be filled by the miracle of experience.

For over five years Mother has sung and danced within my form, slowly filling it with light. It is a song, a play, and miracle is its path; so mysterious, yet with no desire there is no question, only the dance, the moment, the laughter, the joy. So I walk in this realm of dreams, living on the edge of death, but I have already died, and found death to be my best friend. So I walk at peace in his shadow, and let his advice guide my way, while Mother sings eternal, and so graciously blesses my footsteps.

Echo From Pegadeer

The day has come
to cross over the sea,
my eyes have no vision,
there's nothing left of me;
my tears cannot fall
as I melt into thee,
and no matter how I try,
there's no me left to cry.

Art Plate 2·69 ~ Paradise for Pegadeer ~

Last Will and Testament

I, Richard J. Oddo, being of sound spiritual mind and heart here do make my last testament. I hereby bequeath my soul possession, which is my freedom, and give it to the world as an offering of my love. With all due respect and humility, I wish to share my freedom with all this universe equally, and hope that this gesture of love will raise the level of consciousness to the degree I have made the prayer I call my life. I can only hope that each individual will embody this offering of freedom, and let it show in demonstration as their unique expression of truth, for we each are the spiritual essence of God, and have the opportunity to express this miracle of divinity in any manner dictated by the prayer of our heart.

So as my life slowly ebbs, I can only share that which I have embodied and truly own, that is my freedom, and I give it to you, so that you may use it as a beacon to light your way on the road back to your true home...

October 1989

312

So You Think You Understand Reality

Christ and Buddha sit in composure
on the very edge of the deep abyss.
Laughter is their recognition,
and with delight
they push each other from the lofty cliff,
falling to their death.
And here we desperately stay,
clinging in fear to the precipice.

Oh how easy it is to die,
yet buying a loaf of bread
strains the very fiber
of this universe.
So you think you stand
on solid ground,
well close your eyes
and vision will tell,
that the rain is nothing
but dancing clouds,
carried on an idle wind;
and the sun may be there,
but no effort of yours
can induce its radiant light;
and mountains rise to touch the clouds,
yet you walk in the valley,
fearing the impending flood.

Can you let the wind
carry your laughter to the stars,
and look beyond their light
to that which is the seed?
Must a map be provided
to walk within your own home?
and is waking up
really not dreaming?
I am cold now
and must eat something warm.

The Way of One Warrior

When a spiritual book is written, the author's life becomes of paramount issue to determine the validity of its depth. Since I speak of a distinctive way of living, then it is important that I tell a little about my life, so the reader can discern for themself if I live my words, or merely write my fantasies.

Never has there been a better time, or more conducive place to be free — right now, right here — this is my warcry, and my call to freedom. My way of life is in simplicity of living. I have built a small home on wheels — a remodeled van with a raised roof and 15 windows and skylights. It is serene and full of love, and while in my temple I'm surrounded by the glories of nature. I move slowly around the western states, picking a new looping course each year. The variety of scenery out my windows is astonishing, and I have thoroughly explored every type of terrain the West so graciously offers; and after so many years of living within its wild beauty, I have come to know this land well and love it deeply. I hike nearly every day, and also every night, into the primitive lands of this vast country, traversing about 2,000 miles each year on and off trails, exploring the rugged, magnificent terrain of the wilderness on its terms.

Occasionally I visit a small town for a few supplies, but my attempt is at self sufficiency. I grow much of my food in my van, mainly sprouts and greens, and make some of my clothing, and built the van from scratch, including every item in it. I've versed myself in most practical trades (gardening being my favorite), so that I can help and share as I travel, and have acquired skill at many forms of art and physical expression. I am quite sociable, but out in the isolated areas of nature's beauty, there are few souls to commune with. Even though I travel alone, my eyes are turned inward, and my heart is ever joyous in communion with nature and remembrance of my soul, so there is no loneliness.

I own no home, property, animals or people, and the few simple possessions I need are all contained in my van. I have no permanent address, phone, bills or consistent place to visit. I am unattached to the few possessions I have, and feel no pulling desire to travel or remain in one spot, for my spirit is free and takes this body with it. I love life, but have no desire to cling to it, thus my body is on friendly terms with my death.

I have no age, and my name is merely for your convenience, and take full responsibility for my health and all my actions. I belong to no spiritual organization or group, or to any segment of society, and watch no television, nor listen to the radio, nor read newspapers or magazines. I own no clock or make any plans, but let the surrounding circumstances dictate my actions, and allow the weather to dictate the course of my travels. I have nothing pending in my life, and no where I need go, so consequently I'm not in any hurry. I have no path, goal or expectations, thus I am free and unattached to the objects

315

and situations surrounding me.

I'm ever alert to share whenever the situation presents itself, but I do not go looking for the opportunity. I have nothing to give anyone, and nothing to ask of anyone, but I love to share what my spirit dictates, without expectation, desire or attachment, and then move along. If any of my experiences prove beneficial to others, then I am joyous to share, but if not, then I will continue my solitary sojourn within the realm of my heart. I am exuberantly alive, happy, joyous and free.

I wish you peace... LOVE 12

My roots have wheels and the clouds love to laugh, and I must follow their echo...

The author in his home ~ Photo taken by Swami Ganeshananda, a fellow warrior, at Sacramento Vedanta Society ~ Jan. 89 ~

Lapse of The Wind

This strong wind keeps on blowing,
its bound to move me on,
yet today I feel the urge to stay.
But as soon as I sit,
Mother brings out the rain,
well at least the winds have died away.
As long as these mountains
still look new to me,
then I guess I'll be traveling on.
But one day every peak
will look all the same,
and each canyon will hold nothing new.
Only then can I stop
this wayward course & walk,
and perhaps my heart will finally rest.
But for now each rainbow
still brings me delight,
and each corner anticipation awaits.
So this strong wind will keep blowing,
though I don't know why,
perhaps its my laugh gone wild.

My Welcome

Eons and eons ago there was a dream, or perhaps it was but a few decades, and I be one who has not forgotten. The ideals still ring as pounding rhythm to give a beat to the wings of my heart, and freedom they bestow in my gentle footfall. Are there any who remember those days of laughter, where innocence bespoke sincere intent – has the Earth swallowed this bubbling joy, or do exuberantly you walk shadowed in reaches beyond the touch of darkened hope. Step forward if you will; I would share a joyous moment, struck by eternity's hand, with those whose respect has earned humility, and still shine with hope undampened. My book is my welcome, but love must not burden; so I wait in the patience of my heart, for those rare souls who still remember to cast their welcome upon the wind, and share their love with a wandering soul who stands bare as a warrior in spirit.

Final Comment

Nothing is final. Finality means the end of your path, and all paths are illusion. There is only this now and present moment, and the totality of it is right here, all else is concept. The end of a path, or the death of life has never existed, only a constant renewing and reordering of existing energy within a realm of mystery. You are blessed to be on a never ending, perpetually evolving, miraculous adventure of experience. What greater challenge could you ask for, what greater freedom could you receive. The warrior calls this 'the road to nowhere'...

Love
12
Nov~89

To My Family

This book can only vaguely represent who I was, when I wrote it, for a book is only an edifice to a dead idea — nothing is stable. Life proceeds, and the book itself is the evolutional vehicle for the author, and its validity holds its greatest value in his unfoldment to realization. I am who I am, right now and right here — everything else is my shadow of illusion ~

For those who have love in their heart, and respect in their soul, I provide an address for you to correspond with me, and share the communion of your spirit. I sincerely welcome all letters from those who are dedicated to living in greater awareness, but please do not waste our precious, irretrievable time by writing to me about the triviality of the world, for my life is totally dedicated to spiritual realization alone ...

Richard J. Oddo
P.O. Box 7012
Halcyon, Ca. 93421

Within this universe the suns light the void, yet seldom collide — may we sit in joyous communion within the gazebo once again ...

320